Fifteen seconds went by. Or twenty... was hard to keep track.

Her feelings were like the cotton candy they sold in bags on the midway. Delicious but delicate. They would melt away in a second.

She released him and stepped back, pushing him away with light fingers.

"What are you doing, Jack?"

"Unless I'm dreaming, that was a hug. And it was the best part of my day."

"We can't," she said.

"We were."

She held her hand up in a stop-the-car gesture. "This was a mistake. It's late. We're both giddy and tired."

"Didn't feel like a mistake to me," Jack said.

"Hugging the boss is a mistake for me. Tomorrow morning you're the man who owns all this and I'm just a vendor for the summer."

"So?"

She cocked her head to the side and raised an eyebrow. "Maybe you didn't notice, but vendors aren't exactly in the first-class cabins on your ship."

Reader,

Thank you for picking up *Under the Boardwalk*. I hope you enjoy it! This book is dear to my heart because I love amusement parks, the sound of a carousel and summer love. During four summers back in college, I worked at an amusement park just like Starlight Point. While there, I grew up, had fun, indulged my crazy passion for roller coasters and met the love of my life. I still live near the park that inspired Starlight Point, and my husband and I enjoy going there with our children. I'm happy they love roller coasters, too!

I hope reading this book evokes a happy memory of sunshine, carousels and cake. I plan to bring you more stories from Starlight Point in the near future. In the meantime, please visit me at amiedenman.com, find me on Twitter, @amiedenman, or email me at author@amiedenman.com.

Happy reading,

Amie Denman

HEARTWARMING

Under the Boardwalk

Amie Denman

Recycling programs
for this product may
not exist in your area.

ISBN-13: 978-0-373-36774-0

Under the Boardwalk

This edition published by arrangement with Harlequin Books S.A.

For questions and comments about the quality of this book, please contact us at CustomerService@Harlequin.com.

Printed in U.S.A.

Amie Denman lives in a small town in her native Ohio with her husband and sons. She is the author of seven published contemporary romances—all of which take place by the water. Reading books was her favorite escape as a child, and growing up four houses away from the community library encouraged her addiction. When she's not reading or writing, she enjoys gardening, biking and going for walks with her husband. The helpless victim of a lifetime of curiosity, she's been known to chase fire trucks on her bicycle just to see what's going on. Amie believes that everything is fun: especially roller coasters, wedding cake and falling in love. You can find Amie on Twitter, @amiedenman.

To my sons, Joseph and David, who love sunshine and roller coasters as much as I do.

CHAPTER ONE

GUS BACKED HER van down the narrow kitchen driveway at Bay Pavilion Banquet Hall. She was blocking an older SUV parked illegally along the waterfront, but she didn't have time to feel guilty about it. The wedding reception was two hours away, just enough time to stack the cake and pipe it to perfection.

She pulled on her apron, an embroidered cake with a glossy bride and groom covering the top half. Two small bells stitched to the upper straps jingled when she walked.

The early-evening sun slanted off her van's elaborate paint job. Every square inch was pink. *Aunt Augusta's Bakery* swirled in gold metallic lettering across an ornate wedding cake. When she'd pulled in with the new van a few weeks ago, her employees had raised their eyebrows and clamped their mouths shut. All except her aunt Augusta. *She* had snapped a picture with her cell phone and beamed it to her entire list of contacts.

Gus loaded three round cakes on a steel cart, propped open the double side doors to the reception room with her foot and rolled through. When she hurried back for the other two layers, a long shadow darkened the blacktop on the other side of the open van door.

"Cake coming through," she called out. "Make way or suffer the consequences."

She expected to see a catering staffer as she folded the door shut and swung around the side of the van. Instead, a tall man wearing a half wet-suit stood there dripping onto the asphalt. He clutched an oar as if he were preparing to vanquish the mighty pink van.

Gus looked him over from head to toe. Dark brown hair shoved back from his face. Deep brown eyes. High forehead. An amazing four inches taller than her five foot eleven. Slim, athletic build. Huge ticked-off frown.

She stopped the cart, stepped in front of it and grabbed a rubber spatula from her apron pocket. Holding the cooking utensil in front of her, she spread her feet and locked eyes with the wet-suit man.

His lips twitched and his shoulders relaxed.

"I'm pretty good with this spatula," Gus said, her small grin matching his. "You should save yourself and run while you have the chance."

"I'm thinking," he said.

"About putting down the oar and holding those kitchen doors for me?"

"Nope. About the last time I ran away from a woman wielding a spoon."

"It's not a spoon," she said, twirling the spatula in a figure eight.

"My mother's was," he said, stepping back a few inches but still clutching his oar. "A wooden spoon. And she was looking to teach me a lesson with it."

"Cooking lesson?"

He laughed. "I wish. My mother can't cook. It was more of a manners lesson. I'd made fun of my grandmother's ugly couch, and my mother made sure I couldn't sit on it for a week."

"I like your mother already," Gus said, "and I'm sure you have excellent manners as a result of her instruction." She tucked the spatula back in her pocket, and the movement made the wedding bells on her apron jingle. “Does this mean you plan to hold the doors for me?”

He eyed the cake painted on the side of the van and then his gaze swung to the cart behind her.

“Does it come with free cake?”

“Sorry. This one’s for the bride and groom.”

“Will helping make you get your van out of my way faster?”

“Am I in your way?”

“You’re taking up the whole driveway,” he said. “I’d like to load my kayak and get out of here before sundown.”

“I might have a wooden spoon in the van,” she said.

He exhaled loudly. “Fine. I’ll get the doors.”

Gus rolled the cart behind the man in the wet suit. *Attractive*, she thought. *Nice hint of a smile.* But he appeared to be on a mission. She was on a tight schedule, too. The wedding reception was now one hour and forty-five minutes away. If everything went as planned, she’d be fine. But handsome strangers were not part of the plan.

Inside, she placed the largest round layer in the center of the cake table, which was decorated with a pristine tablecloth and a gleaming silver knife. She picked up the next layer, carefully turning it so the design would match the bottom layer, and eased it onto the anchor cake. Stacking a wedding cake was in her blood, a skill she'd inherited from her aunt Augusta and hoped to build a business on. If only running a business were as easy as running a perfect line of piped frosting.

Several servers dressed in classic black and white milled around fussing with tablecloths. They placed silverware on other tables in the elegant reception room and glanced pointedly at her, eyeing the space she was taking up with her cart and cake tools. Apparently *everyone* was in a hurry.

"Do you plan to stand there and watch me?" she asked the stranger. She wondered if he was hoping for a handout. Maybe he'd never seen Martha Stewart on TV and was enthralled watching Gus create a wedding cake.

"I'm waiting for you to move your van." He rolled his shoulders and stretched.

Oh. So much for enthralled.

"It'll be a minute. I have to get the three top layers off the side table. The servers want to set that table and they don't like waiting."

"Neither do I," he said.

Gus picked up the middle cake, its small pink flowers arranged in a crosshatch design. She held it over the layer below as she gauged the perfect placement.

"If you don't want to be inconvenienced, you should be more careful where you park," she said. "You're stopped in the access road for the kitchen."

"No one ever complained before."

Gus took her eyes off the cake and gave him a tight smile. She was trying to practice restraint. He was attractive but appeared uncomfortable, his wet suit making a funny contrast with the formal linens. He resembled an oak tree accidentally planted among fussy flowering shrubs.

The stranger planted one end of his oar on the carpet and leaned on it. Gus lowered the fourth layer into place. She had to focus on the wedding cake that would bring over a thousand bucks into her shop's cash drawer. A drawer that barely had change for a fifty.

"If you give me your keys, I'll move your van myself," he offered.

Gus stepped back to survey the cake. She grabbed a chair from a nearby table and stepped onto it to look down at the four layers she'd stacked so far.

"Are you kidding?" she asked. "How do I know you don't plan to steal it?"

His half laugh turned into a cough. "No risk of that. It's too..."

"What?"

"You know," he said, gesturing as though he could catch the appropriate words.

"Too pretty?" she asked. "Too large? Too powerful for you to handle?"

He cracked his knuckles. "Lady, I'm cold and tired. I'd like to get home."

Gus stepped down from the chair and faced him. "Keys are in the van."

He shot her an unreadable look. Without a word, he turned and strode through the door.

Gus placed the top layer and piped neat borders around the bottoms of each circle, meshing the layers together and bringing the whole cake into focus. Small spring flowers dotted the snowy landscape of white icing and piped designs. Pink rosebuds, yellow daffodils and purple sweet peas trailed over the sides. Perfect for a wedding on the first weekend of May. She dug a camera out of her plastic toolbox and took careful pictures from several angles. It would make a nice addition to her catalog of cakes. Maybe even a portrait for the wall of her bakery.

She rolled her aching shoulders and realized she was mimicking the tall stranger with the wet suit. He was probably long gone by now. She just hoped he hadn't decided her new van—although pink—was nicer than his old SUV. Just her luck, he was on the highway right now with his kayak bumping around in the back of her bakery truck.

When she left the kitchen, the first thing she noticed was her pink van glowing in the early-evening light. It was parked in *almost* the same location. But the other vehicle was not. The owner had managed to extricate the ugly brown-and-tan SUV, and it now sat at the top of the access road.

Blocking her van.

The tall man leaned on an old wooden railing along the bay. His trim frame was silhouetted against the sunset and the lights of the amusement park across the water.

Gus stowed her cake tools and slammed the back doors of the van, hoping the noise would inspire the kayaker to leave. She wanted to unload the van, clean her pastry bags and get to bed before midnight for the first time this week. Gus took off her apron and tossed it on the passenger seat near a small box of cookies. Her shop was testing new recipes for sugar cookies, and she'd brought home three different kinds for the weekend.

She took a second look at the white bakery box on the front seat. One corner was open.

She scrutinized the contents.

Cookies were definitely missing.

JACK TRIED TO think of something clever to say as the owner of the pink van approached. There was no good reason for hanging around. He'd pulled off his wet suit and slipped into worn jeans and an old Starlight Point sweatshirt. The ragged gray shirt had a stretched-out collar and frayed cuffs. The skyline of the amusement park was barely visible after dozens of washings. But it was his favorite sweatshirt, and he felt more comfortable in his own skin when he had it on.

She stopped and leaned on the rail next to him. Without the pink apron, her graceful curves caught his attention and his breath. She was unusually tall, probably just shy of six feet. And although his world was definitely upside down these days, he was sure of one thing. He'd never seen her before.

She looked him right in the eye, a quizzical grin lifting the corners of her mouth.

"Are you Aunt Augusta?" he finally asked.

Probably a few years younger than he was, she wasn't anything like his matronly aunts he saw twice a year at family parties. Her long brown hair was pulled back, revealing her whole face. Fair skin, delicately arched eyebrows. Her eyes were shadowed by the late-afternoon sun behind her, but he remembered their color. Green.

"Which one did you eat?" she asked.

"Which one what?"

"Don't deny it. You've got cookie crumbs on your face."

"The carousel horse."

"Ah," she said. "That's a good design. Only three colors, but the Florentine pattern on the saddle really makes it."

"It reminds me of something."

She glanced at his sweatshirt. "Ever been to Starlight Point?" she asked.

He coughed. "Quite a few times." Like, every day of his life for almost twenty-seven years. He glanced across the bay. The lights were coming on at the amusement park. Starlight Point occupied the entire peninsula separating the bay from the larger lake. Although the park wouldn't open for another two weeks, the lights on the roller coasters glittered in anticipation.

"The carousel-horse cookie is patterned after a horse on the midway carousel."

"Nice idea," he said.

"Thanks. I love that place."

Everybody loved Starlight Point, Jack thought. Especially when roads got paved and taxes poured into Bayside's city coffers from the largest tourist draw in the area.

"How about the cookie's flavor? The frosting?" she asked.

"Loved them both. Very sweet," he said, turning back to look at her and moving closer. "Perfect."

"I was planning to see if the perfection would last, see how it would taste tomorrow at this time. Longevity is a serious bakery issue. Have to keep it fresh or people won't want it."

"Lucky for you I didn't eat them all," he said.

"Lucky for you I'm more flattered than angry."

"I'm glad."

"So," she said. "I thought you were in a big hurry. Didn't you have someplace to be?"

Jack propped a foot on the rail and gazed at the amusement-park lights. The lights on the rides he now owned. Two weeks ago, his father's sudden death stunned his family. Jack's steady orbit around his father had been brought to an agonizing halt. Every day since had sped up like a scrambler ride and Jack wished he could just get off.

He shoved away from the rail. "There's a thousand places I need to be right now," he said, reaching in his pocket for keys.

Maybe tonight was the night to crack open the good bottle of whiskey a friend had given him after his father's funeral. He wanted to run for the safety of his twelve-year-old car.

"Good night," he said abruptly. He walked straight to his SUV, got in the driver's seat and shoved his keys in the ignition. They didn't fit. What the heck? He flipped on the interior light. In his hand was a key attached to a pink-and-gold ceramic wedding cake.

Her door slammed. In two seconds, she'd be at his window.

"First my cookie, now my keys?" She leaned

in his open window and grinned. “Next you’ll be stealing my heart.”

She grabbed her keys, spun and disappeared. He dug deep in his pocket for his own set, waited a second until he heard her engine start, then rolled over his ignition and headed home.

CHAPTER TWO

JACK HAMILTON STRIPPED off his suit jacket, rolled his sleeves and dug through the toolbox bolted to the side of the blue maintenance truck.

"Find it?" Mel Preston yelled. He was almost one hundred feet over Jack's head, perched on the Sea Devil coaster. The navy blue track had white crests of paint at the top of each hill that looked like ocean waves. If all went well, the Sea Devil would whip and spin and make riders feel as if they were in the clutches of a leviathan. And the new ride would bring in enough ticket revenue to justify its staggering cost.

Jack, still digging through the metal box, the morning sun in his eyes, didn't answer right away.

"It's painted red, should have a gauge on it," Mel shouted. He started down the narrow metal steps on the side of the track used for maintenance and emergencies.

Jack pulled tools from the box and stacked them on the tailgate.

"I'm almost at the bottom and I don't think it's..." Something furry brushed his fingers and then crawled over his hand. He jerked his hand out and took a wild step backward.

"Find my pet spider?" Mel asked, breathing heavily after his climb.

Jack leaned against the side of the truck and closed his eyes. He muttered something he knew his longtime friend would ignore.

Mel poured coffee from a thermos into a disposable cup. "Don't know if it's the same spider or the tenth generation. Forgot she's always in there. Named her Black Velvet." He opened a toolbox on the other side of the truck and held up a red gauge. "Here it is. Guess I told you the wrong side."

"Numskull," Jack said, accepting the coffee. "Can't decide if I want to fire you or have this truck sprayed. Or both."

Mel sat on the tailgate, swinging his feet and sipping coffee right out of the thermos.

"That's no way to talk to your favorite employee. I might cry myself to sleep tonight."

"How long till opening day?" Jack asked. "Twelve days?"

"Yep." Mel shaded his eyes and glanced up. "Sea Devil should be ready to go. Just gotta get these hydraulic brakes to pass muster with the state inspectors."

Jack nodded, looking over the coaster and saying nothing. Maintenance trucks littered the grounds at Starlight Point. The midway resembled a carnival parking lot with the food vendors moving into their stands, employees scuttling everywhere to ramp up for what had to be a profitable season. *Had* to be. He thought of what would happen if the family-owned park didn't turn a sizable profit. Jack ran his hand through his hair and rubbed his tired eyes with two fingers.

"Maybe I should have saved that bottle of Jack Daniel's to put in your coffee," Mel suggested. He scratched a spot on his jaw and left a trail of black grease. Mel was the same age as Jack, and they'd been friends for twenty years. Mel had worked his way up from seasonal ride mechanic to head of maintenance and knew every nut and bolt on every ride. Now that the whole weight of Starlight Point rested on Jack's shoulders, he needed Mel's expertise and advice more than ever.

"How are your mom and sisters handling your father's sudden passing?" Mel asked.

"About as well as any of us," Jack said. "Can't decide if it's the best or worst timing in the world. Going so sudden like that, only a month before season opening." Jack sipped his coffee. "Threw us all into a tailspin."

Mel nodded and fiddled with the gauge in his hand.

"Then again, running our butts off to get this year going takes our minds off it," Jack said. He leaned an arm on the side rail of the truck bed. For a few seconds, he considered confiding in his friend. If telling someone would make the situation better, he'd do it. Mel was loyal to the Hamilton family and to Starlight Point. The secret would be safe. But there was nothing Mel could do about the loans piled on loans Ford Hamilton had concealed from everyone—even his own son.

"You've been training to run this place your whole life," Mel said. "Probably have a record season. Just wish your dad was alive to see it."

Jack crumpled his empty cup and tossed it in the construction Dumpster under the new ride.

"Me, too."

GUS MURPHY PLACED cookies in her display case and glanced out the gleaming front windows of Aunt Augusta's Downtown Bakery. Her bakery. Starting this shop with the blessing and help of her namesake aunt had been a leap of faith. She hoped coming home to Bayside last October was the right thing to do. With everything riding on her success, forward was the only direction she could go. But it wasn't going to be easy.

A woman with short silver hair stopped on the front sidewalk. She was pulling a red wagon carrying a medium-sized brown, white and black dog, its nose and front paws hanging over the side. The woman left the dog and the wagon outside and came through the door, setting off a cheerful jingling. She dug in her purse and pulled out several envelopes.

"Wanted to deliver these personally," she said, smiling. "Thank-you notes for being so kind when my husband passed. The sweets you sent to the house were much appreciated. Especially by my son, who would live on cookies if he could."

"Sounds like my kind of guy," Gus said.

"Virginia!" Aunt Augusta came through the swinging door from the back of the bakery. She hustled around the counter, her apron a loud mix of color and frosting.

"Got some new turnovers for you to try on for size. Let's sit by the window where you can keep an eye on Betty, just in case the old gal takes off after a bicycle."

Gus went out front and sat next to the wagon on the sunny sidewalk. She'd hoped the wrought-iron table and chairs in front of her window would attract people in need of a coffee and pastry break. But today she was the only person taking advantage. The life of a baker meant early mornings followed by long days on her feet. She stretched her legs and rested her back against the front wall of the building whose mortgage kept her up at night. What had she been thinking? And now her brilliant idea to bolster her immediate cash flow meant she'd divide her time between her bakery and her business venture at Starlight Point.

She groaned. Betty woke up, nose twitching, and licked Gus's hand. "I'll have to wash that later," Gus told Betty. "Who knows where your tongue has been?" She scratched the dog's ears.

Betty licked her palm once more as a long

shadow crossed the sidewalk. Gus glanced up. Way up. The kayaker who liked cookies stood over her. He looked even better in the daylight. And in a button-down oxford with the sleeves rolled to his elbows.

Betty leaped from the wagon and put her paws on the man's knees. He picked her up, ruffling her furry face and ears.

"I'm guessing you and Betty have met before," Gus observed.

"We're old friends."

"You have a lot in common," Gus said. "She's tempted by my cookies, too, and I've caught her trying to steal one."

"Still haven't forgiven me?"

Gus shrugged and smiled. "I was never mad in the first place. I make sweets, people eat them. Sometimes they even pay me. I'm hoping to build a business on that idea."

He glanced at her apron. "Are you taking a break right now?"

She pointed over her shoulder. "Aunt Augusta's in charge at the moment."

He leaned close to the window, looked in and waved. Turning back to Gus, he bent and placed Betty in the wagon.

"You know my aunt?" Gus asked.

"Nope, but I know my mother. I told her I'd pick her up downtown after she delivered her notes."

Betty settled in with a sigh and put her nose on the edge of the wagon where she could see everything, including the door of the shop.

"Since I'm pretty sure we're not cousins, there's only one explanation," Gus said. "If Virginia is your mother, and Betty loves you like family, you must be—"

"Jack Hamilton," he said, extending one large sun-browned hand.

So the impatient kayaker who drove an ancient SUV was the new owner of Starlight Point? Of course she knew about his father's sudden death a few weeks ago—the whole area had been shocked that such a relatively young man had been taken by a heart attack. She had met Ford Hamilton twice to discuss the contract for the three bakeries she would lease at Starlight Point this summer. In her downtown bakery, there had been a lot of speculation about the future of the amusement park, but the counter talk focused on the twenty-six-year-old son who was ready to step in.

Gus had returned to Bayside only last fall to put down roots, but her aunt and Jack's mother were old acquaintances. Although Gus had seen Virginia a number of times over the winter, she hadn't met any of the three Hamilton children.

Until now.

Gus took Jack's hand and pulled herself up. A rush of endorphins whirled through her like a scrambler ride. Maybe it was his smile. Maybe she'd stood up too fast. She held on to his hand.

"Augusta Murphy," she said. "Most people call me Gus."

"Why?"

"When I was young, it was because Gus is a much cuter name than Augusta. These days, I think it's so I don't get confused with Aunt Augusta."

"Who would make that mistake?" he said, grinning and keeping a firm grip on her hand. He inclined his head toward the door of the shop. "Can I buy you a cup of coffee to make up for ruining your cookie experiment?"

"My experiment failed anyway," she said. "I ate the rest of the cookies Saturday night while I watched the TV shows I'd recorded all week."

"All baking and cooking channels?" he asked.

"Nope. I only watch comedies and reality shows that are nothing like actual reality. I can't take television seriously."

"What do you take seriously?" he asked.

"Birthday cake."

He nodded. "Cake can make or break a good party."

"Cake is the star of every birthday party and wedding," she said. "It's the guest of honor."

Gus smiled, liking the way the sun picked up the lighter brown in Jack's dark hair. He smiled back. At that moment, she wondered what it would be like to run her fingers through the hair that waved away from his high forehead.

"Jack," Virginia said as she came out the shop door. "I see you've met the most talented lady in Bayside." Virginia turned to Gus. "He's had a love affair with sugar since he could walk. Used to drive the bakery vendor at the Point nuts all summer."

"He did steal one cookie," Gus said. "Right out of my van."

"I'm not surprised," Virginia replied. "He couldn't help himself, I'm sure. You have to admit, you've got baking in your blood. I was just talking to your aunt about having you be the STRIPE sergeant this summer."

Aunt Augusta stood in the doorway behind Virginia, hands held out in a gesture of innocence, eyes huge.

"STRIPE?" Gus asked, raising an eyebrow at Jack.

"You don't want to know," he said, leaning close to her as his mother turned to say good-bye to Aunt Augusta. "But whatever she asks you to do, I suggest you say no." He wrinkled his brow and leaned back, cocking his head. "Wait a minute. Are you working at Starlight Point this summer?"

"Yes. Didn't you know? I…"

Virginia sailed between them, took Jack's arm with one hand and grabbed the wagon's handle with the other. Jack stared at Gus as if he was trying to figure out a puzzle, but his mother's momentum tugged him away.

"We'll talk," Virginia said over her shoulder. "Later. I need a strong woman for my mission."

Betty's sleepy glance lingered on Gus as

she rode in the wagon behind Virginia and Jack Hamilton. Jack turned and looked back, too, and Gus wondered what it would be like to see him every day at Starlight Point.

CHAPTER THREE

GUS PARKED IN front of her bakery on the Starlight Point midway. The wide concrete avenue had snack and souvenir shops down both sides with skyway cars running overhead. A few rides and a theater were mixed in among the shops, most notably a historic carousel right in front of her bakery's new pink awning.

The back of the van, usually outfitted for transporting wedding cakes, held three large convection ovens. One for each of the bakeshops Gus was leasing for the summer. She had another location in the Wonderful West and one in the Lake Breeze Hotel.

Last year the Point's baker retired only weeks before Gus came home to Bayside. It seemed like a sign from the baking universe that she should make the leap. Now, though, with the sudden death of Ford Hamilton, she needed to get the paperwork in order to confirm the verbal contract they'd negotiated. Not usually the nervous sort, Gus wondered what changes Jack Hamilton might make.

She opened her van doors and stared at the ovens, hands on hips. She glanced at the side door of her bakery.

"How are you planning to unload all that?" The newly familiar voice sent a ripple through her.

Gus had wondered the same thing. Optimism could only get a girl so far. She needed muscle.

And Jack appeared to have plenty of it.

"I'm taking suggestions," she said. She could use all the help she could find. Getting three bakeshops equipped, staffed, supplied and running in the next ten days would be as easy as teaching a cat to shave.

He shrugged off his dark gray suit jacket and slung it over the open van door. Gus thought he should shed the crisp white dress shirt, too, just to be on the safe side. But he rolled up the sleeves instead.

"I'm not busy right now," he said.

Gus laughed. She gestured at the chaos everywhere around them. Maintenance trucks and crews crawled along the midway like ants over ice cream spilled on the sidewalk. Other vendors parked in front of shops and hauled merchandise. The skyway cars groaned into action overhead, shaking off their winter's rest.

"Right," she said. "This place probably runs itself."

Jack looked at the overhead cars and then rubbed his eyes with the heels of both hands. "Sure. How about we trade? I'll put on an apron with those little bells, and you can wear my name tag, which pretty much asks for trouble."

The cell phone in his coat pocket rang, vibrating loudly against the metal van door.

"Are you going to answer that?" she asked.

"Can't. I'm busy helping a vendor I just met. I wondered who would replace our old baker. I grew up stealing sweets from him." He gestured toward the pink awning. "I like the improvement already."

Gus pulled a two-wheeled dolly out of the van. "I'm just getting started. I should have been here weeks ago, but I've been busy with spring wedding season."

"How are you going to manage summer wedding season?"

"One cake at a time," she said as she climbed into the back of the van.

Gus shoved the first boxed oven to the rear and Jack manhandled it onto the cart. She held the door and watched him muscle it right into a corner of her midway bakery.

"Can I talk you into coming to my bakeries in the hotel and the Wonderful West? I still have two ovens in the van."

She figured there was zero chance of this happening. The owner of Starlight Point wasn't likely to waste any more of his countdown-to-opening-day time. Especially since he hardly knew her, but now he knew how heavy those boxes were.

Jack glanced at the wall clock. Its hands were stopped, the unplugged cord swinging beneath it. "Looks like I have plenty of time," he said.

A few of the other vendors waved and then paused, a puzzled expression on their faces as they saw Jack Hamilton toss his suit coat on the floor of the van, shut the back doors and climb in the shotgun seat with Gus at the wheel.

"Do you usually help vendors move in?" she asked.

"There is nothing usual about this year," he said, unrolling his window. "Turn just before the Scrambler and we can squeeze out the beach gate and drive down the boardwalk to the hotel."

It was too early for anyone to be tempted by Lake Huron's cold waters, but lifeguards swept the beach and set up chairs as they passed by.

"I'm sorry about your father," Gus said.

Jack kept his head turned, watching the beach and lake. "Thank you," he said quietly.

Gus wanted to ask how he planned to manage the park and if she would see a contract anytime soon. She regretted the handshake and verbal agreement she'd made with Ford Hamilton. She'd planned to sign the papers a month ago, but then everything changed.

The financial risks she'd taken woke her up in the night, but her problems were nothing compared to Jack's. Losing a parent and gaining a huge family business in one fell swoop? That was a sleep stealer.

"Should be a quick drop-off at the hotel bakeshop. And I bet you know a shortcut through the Wonderful West to my bakery."

"We could take the train," he suggested,

turning to her with a hint of a smile. "But there's a shoot-out on the tracks right behind the Last Chance. I hope you don't mind listening to gunfire all summer."

She laughed. "That wasn't in the contract."

Jack's smile faded and he returned to looking out the window as she maneuvered the van into the hotel's loading dock. He was quiet as they shoved the second box out and deposited it in the bakeshop.

He directed her through a back gate and she drove from the outer loop road straight into the Wonderful West. She dodged queue lines, trees and maintenance trucks as she drove on "The Trail." A tall, slim girl with a messenger bag slung over her shoulder walked along the trail, her back to them.

Suddenly, Jack reached over and blew the van's horn, brushing his fingers over Gus's on the steering wheel.

"My sister," he said, grinning.

Hand over her heart with an expression of surprise mixed with homicide, the tall girl mouthed the word *jerkface* as they passed her.

"That was loud and clear," Gus said.

"Evie loves me. I'm way less irritating than our sister, June."

"Should I stop?"

He shook his head. "Nope. Evie's on a mission right now. And so are we."

"Is she your...um...copresident?"

"No. Still one year left of college. She'll work here for the summer, but just a regular job. Not as an owner. She deserves one more carefree summer."

His voice was low and joyless, like an echo outside a funeral. Was it really so bad owning an amusement park?

"Does Evie like to bake? Maybe she could work for me?" Gus asked.

"I doubt she can bake—she certainly wouldn't have learned from our mom. She's majoring in accounting. Getting her CPA."

"Even better. I might just hire her to manage the accounts for my three shops. I need someone strong I can trust, or I'll never make it."

"I know what you mean," he said.

They pulled up to the Last Chance Bakery and wrangled the final oven across the uneven planked porch. Evie swung through the saloon doors just as they slid the oven into place. She had a beautiful smile and looked a lot like her brother, with a few exceptions.

Her hair was several shades closer to blond and her eyes were almost green.

"I'm Evie," she said, sticking out her hand for Gus to shake. "And I didn't mean *you* were a jerkface. I know who blew that horn."

"I'm glad. And glad to meet you. I was just talking to your brother about snapping you up before someone else does."

"A job?"

"Managing the books for my bakeries here."

"I would love it," she said. "I usually work for a vendor because there's less conflict of interest. Speaking of which," she continued as she rummaged through her bag, "I'm out delivering contracts to all the vendors right now."

"Gotta go," Jack said. "My secretary's called fifteen times and she'll probably get on the PA system if I don't show up."

Without another word, Jack speed-walked across the bakery's porch and headed up the trail to the front of the park. Gus wondered why he'd ignored the phone calls for the past hour, but she imagined there was a lot she didn't know about Jack and his business. Perhaps Evie showing up was the convenient exit he'd been hoping for.

"I'll come by later when I'm done," Evie said. "This is the best job offer I've had. Especially since the airbrushing stand didn't work out last year and I'm no good at scooping ice cream. Numbers I understand."

LATE THAT AFTERNOON, Jack locked the men's room door and leaned against it, eyes closed, for a full minute before heading for the sink. Cold water rushed over his hands as he scrubbed them mercilessly. Warm water would've been better for washing away the grease and construction dust he'd picked up on the latest inspection of the Sea Devil, but he needed to cool off. He stared at the rivers of water rolling over his fingers, imagining all his problems sluicing away.

"Gotta get a grip," he said. Jack dried his hands, smoothed down and buttoned his sleeves, rolled his shoulders. He refused to look at his own face—his father's face, thirty years younger—in the mirror.

Dorothea waited for him outside his office door. Her desk straddled the space between his office and the one that was formerly his father's. No one used Ford Hamilton's office now, leaving Dorothea half-adrift.

"One of the vendors stopped in to see you while you were out on the Sea Devil."

"Which one?"

"Augusta Murphy."

Jack considered Dorothea for a moment. She had to be in her late fifties and had worked for Starlight Point for decades. Maybe if he asked her advice? Maybe she knew all the things his father hadn't told his own son about the way he was doing business. Doubtful.

"Very tall and very pretty."

Jack smiled for the first time in hours.

"She also seemed very mad."

His smile vanished.

"Is she coming back?"

"Wants you to come to her bakery in the hotel. Seems to think she can tell you what to do with your time," Dorothea said. She grinned at Jack. "I thought that was my job."

"I planned to stop by the Lake Breeze this afternoon anyway. I want to see if it's close to being ready for opening weekend. Guess it wouldn't be much out of my way to see what she wants."

"I told her not to count on it."

"Thank you, Dorothea. I'll see what I can do."

WHEN JACK ZIPPED over to the hotel on one of the many loaner employee bicycles they kept all over the Point, he hoped to have a chance to talk to Gus alone. He'd been up late worrying about the vendor contracts. His father had always negotiated those, giving Jack only a vague idea of where that income fit into the general scheme of things. He hadn't even known Aunt Augusta's was replacing the retired baker until he'd grilled his mother over lunch downtown. Sadly, he was beginning to realize his mother had only a cursory idea of how Starlight Point ran.

Looking in from the outside, everyone probably figured he was privy to all his father's business decisions. *If they only knew.* To write up the formal contracts, Jack had researched some boilerplate industry standards, pulled out five years' worth of Starlight Point contracts and run the ideas past the foods manager. Jimmy Henry had raised his eyebrows when Jack wanted to review the fees and profit share from the vendors.

"Never looked at those before," he'd said.

"Your father only asked me when he thought one of them might cut into our sales. Generally, we get the sit-down business and the vendors get the stand-up. Full-service restaurants are ours, snack and drink stands are theirs. Worked that way for years."

"I know, but what do you think of the rent and the percent of the profits we charge? Could we get away with raising them?"

"Search me. Can't speak for any of them and haven't seen their returns. Maybe they've been making out like bandits all these years. Maybe you'll break 'em if you raise the rent and they'll all pull out. Wish I could help you, but I run our sit-downs and only get involved if someone competes with my restaurants," he'd repeated, as if washing his hands of the issue.

"Worried about any of these vendors competing with us?"

"Are they the same ones as last year?"

"All except for the three bakeries. New owner."

Jimmy had shrugged. "Bakers are bakers."

When Jack entered the hotel lobby, he wondered if Jimmy had ever met Gus. Perched on the check-in counter addressing a group of twenty or so people, Gus did not look like an average baker.

The room shifted in his direction when he entered the lobby. His tie was loose, his suit coat flapped and he had a rubber band securing his right pant leg. Like his father, he always wore a suit at work, but getting his pants caught in the bicycle chain two summers ago had been enough to teach him a lesson.

He sat in a plush lobby chair, pulled off his black dress shoe and jerked off the rubber band. Everyone watched him. It was as if the guest of honor had entered a surprise birthday party half an hour before anyone expected him.

Gus strode across the lobby, the group right behind her, and stood so close Jack couldn't get up without looking really awkward. He hadn't gotten his shoe back on, and now he felt exposed, trapped. *Please don't let there be a hole in my sock.* At five foot eleven, Gus was already imposing. And gorgeous. Her eyes were bright, her cheeks flushed, hair a little wild.

"Thank you for coming to our meeting," she said tersely. Each word dripped with ice.

Jack relaxed in the chair, draped an arm

across the back and crossed one leg over the other. His black dress shoe knocked against Gus's shin but neither of them gave an inch. If she wanted to unleash some kind of righteous fury on him about the contract, he wasn't backing down in front of a lobby of vendors.

"Didn't know it was a formal meeting," he said.

"It is now. We want to talk about these terms." She waved the contract at him. The twenty or so other vendors behind her had similar white papers clutched in their fingers. No one looked happy. Even the ones who'd been here for years. Maybe he'd gone too far. But now he was stuck.

"Go ahead," Jack said coolly, his glance returning to Gus's face. "Talk."

She tilted her head and narrowed her eyes. Jack would've liked to tell her she was beautiful when she was angry, but the last thing he wanted was to look flushed in front of a group of ticked-off vendors. Why did Gus have this effect on him and why the heck had she set him up like this? He would have liked a private conversation with her about the lease terms. But this felt more like a sneak attack than a negotiation.

"Twenty thousand for the space and twenty

percent of the profits is not the deal I negotiated with Ford Hamilton last fall," she said.

Other vendors fanned out behind her so they formed a half circle. They nodded in agreement, entrapping Jack in a back-down-or-be-a-butthead situation.

"In case you haven't noticed," he said slowly, "Ford Hamilton is dead. His verbal contracts are null and void."

Several of the vendors—Bernie from Bernie's Famous Boardwalk Fries and Tosha from Tosha's Homemade Ice Cream—gasped and shook their heads. They'd known him since he was a little boy climbing on their counters and begging for free samples. They'd worked with his father for two decades or more. Maybe he was making a mistake…

"So…?" Gus prodded. "You really plan to renege on the deal we all thought we had—ten thousand and ten percent—on a technicality?" The hard lines of her mouth showed no signs of softening. She plucked the rubber band from the arm of his chair and started snapping it with her fingers.

Jack felt her words like a punch to his chest, knocking his breath away and spiking adrenaline through his veins. "My father's death is a lot more than a technicality. If you don't like the deal, don't take it. Nobody's forcing you to sign."

Her mouth dropped open a little and she stepped back. Only a small step, but enough to give him room to stand. He topped her by only four inches, and together they looked like giants in front of a pack of smaller villagers, all angry. Seeing the accusatory faces of the vendors didn't do a thing for Jack's mood. He knew he should save face, make a graceful exit, schedule an actual meeting to discuss the situation. But not now. Hard retreat was the only way his tenuous grasp on his emotions wouldn't crack.

He stared at the lobby wall behind the group, anger, pain and frustration tightening his jaw and spine. He couldn't look them in the eye. Wouldn't. It was going to be a season, maybe several, of tough choices. He'd have to get used to it.

"I'll give you until tomorrow afternoon to sign the new contracts and return them to my office. You are under no obligation to lease space at Starlight Point. If you don't return the signed contracts by this time tomorrow,

I'll assume you're backing out and replace you immediately."

Jack turned and headed for the beach entrance, only pausing a second when he felt the sharp zing of a rubber band on the back of his head as he slid through the doors.

CHAPTER FOUR

TOSHA PUT HER arm around Gus, her head barely reaching Gus's shoulder. "I don't know whether to laugh, cry or turn him over my knee and spank him," she said.

"You got a good aim," the hot-dog vendor said. "I say we elect you as our official leader."

"I'm the newest one here," Gus objected.

"But you've got three bakeries," Bernie said. "And I'll bet you've got as much riding on this season as the rest of us."

Gus thought of the payments on her business loan. No kidding.

"What do we do?" she asked, dropping into the chair vacated by Jack Hamilton. "Tell him to go jump in the lake and take his extra ten thousand and ten percent with him?"

"That'd sure be nice," Hank said. He tugged at his butcher's-style shirt, which had *Hank's Hot Dogs* embroidered on it. "But I was planning on going to Florida this winter with the money I make this summer. Arthritis is getting to my wife."

"If we all walk, he won't be able to replace us in time for opening day, will he?" Gus asked.

The other vendors shifted nervously and exchanged swift glances.

"Probably not right away," Hank said. "It would put the hurt to him for a while at least."

"But he'd replace us eventually and we'd be out," Bernie said. "Permanently."

"Nobody wants to walk away," Tosha said. "This has been our summer home for years. We all loved Jack's father, and those Hamilton kids have practically grown up under our noses. They're like family. Right?"

No one said anything.

"We could try *threatening* to walk away and see what he does," Tosha added.

"I'm afraid he'd let us go. You heard what he said—twenty-four hours to sign the contracts. I'm not so sure bluffing will work on him," Hank said. "His dad was an easy guy to work for, but I wonder about Jack. Can't figure out what's going on in his head now that the whole thing's in his lap."

Gus sighed. "I have all my money riding on these bakeries and the one downtown. I'm in deep."

"I can't afford to pull up stakes," Bernie said. "Besides, people expect me to be here… they bring their kids to get the same boardwalk fries they got when they were little." He spread his hands, looking around him for support. "It's a tradition."

"Hate to bother her when she's grieving, but we could try talking to Jack's mother," Hank suggested.

"No," three voices said at the same time.

"Virginia gets wind of this," Bernie said, "we'll all get etiquette lessons for the STRIPE this summer."

"Lessons?" Gus asked. Virginia had mentioned making Gus her STRIPE sergeant, but she'd let the thought get lost among all her other concerns.

Tosha sat on the arm of Gus's chair. "Every summer, Virginia plans and operates the Summer Training Improvement Program for Employees. All employees. Vendors, management, security, beach patrol, *everyone*."

Hank nodded and grimaced. "Everyone. Part of the contract."

"Is it part of our contract?" Gus asked. She flipped through the document crumpled in her hand.

"Page four," Bernie said. "Already checked."

"So, what does everyone have to do?"

"Depends on the program," Tosha explained. "It's usually a skill Virginia considers useful. She always insists that, whatever her crazy idea is, everyone should know how to do it just in case. She views this as more than just a summer job, wants people to take away skills as well as their minimum wage, I guess."

"I'm almost afraid to ask," Gus said. "What kind of stuff have you had to do?"

"Change the oil in a car engine," Hank said.

"Swimming lessons," Tosha added.

The other vendors jumped in.

"Square dancing."

"Setting a formal dinner table and polishing silver."

"Knitting socks and a scarf."

"Conversational Spanish."

"Riding a horse—English and Western."

Gus felt her tension slipping into the soft chair. She grinned. "I had no idea this job came with such perks. I feel like a better person already."

Bernie groaned. "You gotta understand. Virginia's serious about this stuff. You not only have to attend a series of classes, but you gotta prove you actually paid attention." He passed a large hand over his face. "Didn't think I was going to make it the summer we had to sew a backpack and embroider our name on it. To her satisfaction." He looked around, a lopsided grin edging up one corner of his mouth. "You know what? I still use that darn thing."

"How can this be legal?" Gus asked. "It seems pretty far-fetched."

Hank shrugged. "If it's in the contract and you sign it, you're obligated. If you don't play along, you're not getting invited back next year."

"Assuming we make it through this year," Tosha said.

"Maybe I can help," Gus said. "Virginia said something about me being a sergeant this year. What if she wants everyone to learn to bake chocolate-chip cookies? I could make it easy for you."

"No way," Hank said. "It wouldn't be that

simple. We probably have to assemble a three-tiered wedding cake and deliver it. Just in case we ever need to do that in our lives."

"Or make a soufflé that doesn't fall, even in a thunderstorm," Tosha suggested.

"Or decorate cookies representing every ride in the ever-lovin' park," Hank growled.

"Hope not," Gus said. "I've got some signature cookies planned, even ordered special cutters in the shapes of some of the trademark rides. Don't want anyone stealing my thunder."

Everyone was silent for a moment.

"So," Tosha said. "Sounds like you plan to sign that contract and stick it out?"

Gus fooled with the silver *A* she wore on a chain around her neck. "I've got three shops."

"That's sixty thousand bucks," Bernie said. "He's killing you worse than the rest of us."

"But I've already made a huge investment in equipment, got supplies ordered. I'm in debt up to my eyebrows." Gus tucked a lock of hair behind her ear and looked up, meeting the eyes of the more vocal vendors standing closest to her. "If I walk away, I lose for sure. If I stay, it's a gamble."

"We could try talking to him again," Hank

suggested. "Maybe not gang up on him this time. He's probably still smarting from everything that's happened."

Gus raised one eyebrow, twisting her necklace and chewing her lip. Hank had ketchup and mustard stains permanently occupying his shirtfront, but he had a point.

"I think we should send you," Bernie said, pointing at Gus.

"Why me?"

"I agree," Tosha said. "Since you're the newest of us, you've got a more practical approach. Not so much emotional baggage."

Gus considered her connection to Jack so far. She'd met him for the first time Saturday night in the parking lot. Standing next to him by the darkening bay, she'd felt a tug of...something.

"Plus you've got three stores here," Hank said. "You're a great choice for spokesman."

"And you're the tallest," Bernie added, smiling.

"Very convincing," Gus said.

They all waited for her to say something.

"I'll try to talk to him later today," Gus said. "I'm interviewing workers for my bakeshops in about fifteen minutes."

Gus followed the same path of retreat Jack had taken only ten minutes before. The Lake Breeze Hotel was aptly named: its location on the lakeside of the Starlight Point Peninsula opened it to fresh air all year long. A wide sandy beach and a boardwalk were the only things between the massive Victorian structure and the water.

She leaned on the blue metal railing separating the boardwalk from the sandy beach. Bright sunshine and the sparkling lake should have made her happy, but she had a sixty-thousand-dollar lump in her throat. How could she manage it?

Movement way down the deserted boardwalk caught her eye. She turned her head just enough to see Jack Hamilton doing exactly the same thing she was. He leaned on the railing, stared at the sunshine and water, and didn't look any happier than she did.

Gus considered marching down the boardwalk and negotiating the terms of all the lease vendors' contracts right then and there. She'd go with honey, not vinegar, this time in hopes of catching something a whole lot more pleasant than the deal they had right now. She'd toss her hair, smile winningly and appeal to his soft side. If he had one.

She took one step. Two steps. And thought better of it. He was brooding. Maybe he was grieving for his father. Overwhelmed by his new responsibilities? Or secretly delighted he finally had the power to profit from people like her, Hank, Tosha and Bernie? Maybe he wanted to drive the vendors out and keep all the cash from the food stands. Whatever his deal was, Gus didn't think approaching him now would help the vendors' cause. Especially since he could probably guess who'd snapped a rubber band into his cranium only minutes before. Time might be her friend when it came to figuring out how to deal with Jack Hamilton.

GUS WAS BEAUTIFUL. And she'd be right under his nose all summer long. Unless he chased her away with his asinine contract hikes.

The sound of a maintenance cart zooming down the boardwalk reminded him of what he was supposed to be doing right now. He glanced up and grinned. Mel Preston bore down on him like a storm from the Northeast, gunning the cart for all it was worth. He whipped past Augusta, nearly clipping her.

Jack pulled off his suit coat and slung it over his shoulder.

"Roll up your sleeves, boss," Mel yelled over the rattling of the ancient cart. "You're going up on the Sea Devil with me."

"Problem?"

"State inspectors. One hour. They're several days early. They claim it's just a preliminary, but I don't want to take chances."

"Are we ready? Think we'll pass?"

"We're gonna try. Get in."

Jack tossed his jacket in the back of the cart, sat on the cracked vinyl seat next to his best friend and jerked off his tie while Mel whipped the cart around and headed back in the direction he'd come from. They breezed by Augusta, only inches away, and Jack's eyes briefly met hers. It was probably a good thing he wouldn't have time to talk about the contract today. The next time they met, it would be on his terms. No angry villagers with pitchforks waving contracts and snapping him with rubber bands.

Jack twisted around in the seat and looked back at Gus. She stood by the railing, facing him. He was getting farther and farther away, but he knew she was watching him. He finally turned and faced forward, trying to put the image of her, with the sun and water behind her, out of his head.

"Heck of a good-looking woman," Mel said.

"Looks like trouble to me."

"Know her?"

Jack nodded. "She owns Aunt Augusta's Bakery. Makes cookies you'd kill for. Gonna operate three vendor shops here this summer."

"I saw the signs in the warehouse. Our guys will put 'em up later this week."

"If she signs her contract by tomorrow afternoon."

"She hasn't signed yet? Season starts in ten days."

"None of the vendors have officially signed."

"Thought your dad handled all that before... you know."

Jack unbuttoned his cuffs and rolled his sleeves. "My father left quite a few loose ends when he died. I had to draw up the contracts myself. I changed some of the terms, and the vendors aren't too happy with me right now. Especially one particular baker."

Mel glanced over then resumed navigating the rear gate from the hotel area to the back of the Sea Devil. “Never been interested in your business affairs and contracts and such, but I figure you’ve inherited about as much as you can handle.”

“Wish I could tell you you’re wrong.”

Mel laughed. “You love it when I’m wrong.”

“Makes me feel smarter. And right now, I need all the help I can get.”

Mel parked the cart under the new ride. “Wish the inspectors weren’t showing up early, but I think we’re ready. This ride’s been a long time in the works, and we’ve just got a few details to finalize before it’ll be safe enough for your china dinner plates.”

“Nice to know you’ve been earning that generous salary.” Jack punched Mel lightly on the shoulder as they stepped out of the cart and headed for the steel ladder extending from the steps on the first hill of the coaster.

“Doubt you could pay me what I’m worth, but you’re welcome to try,” Mel said.

“Let’s see how the inspection goes. I’ve got a lot riding on the Sea Devil.”

If only Mel knew just how much.

CHAPTER FIVE

AFTER A MARATHON session making wedding-cake flowers, Gus stood at her shop door ready to flip the sign to Closed. A tall man loitered outside. He met her eyes but didn't move a muscle.

She stared back, waiting to see if he would make the first move.

Or any move.

Gus caved first, stepped back and pulled the door open.

"Can I help you?"

"Are you closed?" Jack asked.

"Closing," she said, managing a small smile until she remembered the thirty-thousand-dollar kick in the gut he'd delivered a few days ago.

"I just..." He stopped. Gus wanted to put him at ease—her natural inclination was to be the sunshine in the rain, especially in the doorway of her own business. She glanced at her apron and fiddled with the knot in front. It was fully decked out in summery designs. Beach chairs, fireworks, bikinis, a flag, a boat.

Jack gestured to her apron. "I like it," he said.

Gus said nothing, trying for a neutral expression and hoping he would go away. She was the official spokesperson for the lease vendors at the Point, who were getting a rotten deal from the six feet three inches of man standing in front of her. She squared her shoulders and tried not to think of him as an attractive man with a sweet tooth and a smile that could melt chocolate.

"Summer is my favorite season," he said. He looked pointedly at all the symbols on her apron. "I like all of those things."

One hundred percent awkward.

He shifted his feet and propped the door open with his hand. "Maybe you could put the Sea Devil on an apron to wear at the Point this summer."

Gus had broken her own record. She hadn't kept her mouth shut for this long since she'd gotten her wisdom teeth out in high school.

Jack stepped into the open doorway now, preventing her from slamming the door in his face and locking it.

"I saw that you signed the contract," he ventured. "All the vendors did."

Gus tried to relax her jaw. What was the point of his visit? To gloat? She untied her apron, pulled it over her head and hung it on the back of a nearby chair.

"We didn't have much choice," she finally said.

"Yes, you did."

Gus started arranging chairs around the small tables in the front of the shop. Four chairs per table, perfectly spaced and shoved in. There was something satisfying about keeping her hands busy and her back to Jack. She could not look at him. Would not give him the satisfaction. He was on her turf here. He was the one who should be uncomfortable. She aligned the chairs viciously, snapping them into place with their shoulders pinned against the tables.

He approached the glass case and looked at the cookies and cakes on display.

"What I mean is," he said, "you did have a choice."

Gus crossed her arms over her chest and faced him. She wanted to get behind her counter, her shield, her fortress of confections—but he blocked her way to the pass-through.

"You could have told me to go jump in the lake with my contract," he continued, a small grin sliding up one side of his face.

"I thought about it," Gus said. She'd thought about him quite a lot, as a matter of fact.

He chuckled. "I'm sure you did."

Gus exhaled slowly. "Sorry if I don't find it so funny."

"It's not. It's business. Nothing funny about business."

"Says the man who owns an amusement park."

He continued to gaze at the cookies in the case. No way was she offering him one now. Even if it would make him go away.

Gus wondered if her aunt was listening to this conversation. Aunt Augusta had helped her all day and should be washing up. Gus should hear water running, but no sounds came from the kitchen.

Jack suddenly stepped closer and looked down at her. He smelled like a man who'd been outside all day, a hint of lake air and a touch of sweat. It was a nice combination. Too nice. She had to keep her mind on her business, which was currently a house of cards built on bank loans and confectioner's sugar.

"I would have been in a real bind if you'd all refused to sign. Don't know how I would've replaced you all at such short notice."

Gus wanted to throw something. What was wrong with this guy?

"I'm just so glad we didn't inconvenience you," she said, her words laced with bitterness. "I'm sure you're hoping we'll all make a nice profit and your twenty percent—instead of the original ten—will be even sweeter."

"Of course I hope so."

Gus stared wordlessly at him. Heat crept over her; her ears flamed. She made a Herculean effort to keep her voice from shaking.

"I have work to do," she said abruptly, clipping off the words and hoping they conveyed dismissal.

"I thought you were closing for the day," he said.

With a genius like him at the helm of Starlight Point, we're all in serious trouble. Has he never seen a bakery kitchen after it was closed for the day?

Maybe he didn't know the first thing about actual work. But she did. She grabbed her apron off the back of a chair and folded it. Jack moved toward the door, leaving the floor open for Gus to retreat behind her counter. She felt braver there, like a judge behind a bench.

"I'll go," Jack said. "I just stopped by to say…"

Gus tapped a pencil on the counter while she waited. It was funny to see such a tall, well-dressed man acting so… What was it? Nervous? Guilty? Aloof?

"I know how influential you are with the other vendors," he said, looking her directly in the eyes. "Honestly, I don't know why."

"You don't know why people would listen to me." It was a statement, not a question. Of course he wouldn't get it. She kept her voice steady. "I'm the newest one there and a mere…"

"Baker?" Jack supplied. "That's one of my favorite professions."

Gus wanted to laugh, if only to break the tension. Her shoulders were like wild dogs straining at the leash of her spinal column.

"Let me enlighten you. The other vendors asked me to speak for them because I have three locations at Starlight Point. My sixty thousand dollars carries a lot of weight with them and with me."

"So why didn't you?"

"What?"

"Speak for them?" he said. "I thought you might come at me without the oven mitts."

"I did come by the next morning, but your troll of a secretary said you were unavailable and would be all day. She implied I was wasting my time even trying."

"Dorothea has been with us for centuries. She's very loyal."

"I'll have to name a cookie after her."

"She'd like that."

Gus rolled her eyes and continued, "So did you really tell your guard not to let me past the palace gate?"

"It's a busy time of year," Jack said.

"Um, you gave us twenty-four hours to make a decision that could make or break our businesses. And you couldn't make time to negotiate? Really?"

Jack stared at his shoes, his shoulders sagging. "I am sorry I didn't get a chance to see you."

"And what would you have done if you had?" Gus asked hotly. "Renegotiated? Offered us a better deal? Honored your father's verbal commitment to people he'd worked with for years—some of them for decades?" She knew she was stepping over a line, invoking his deceased father, but he'd invaded her shop and insulted her.

Jack stared at her for ten long seconds, the veins standing out in his neck.

"I wouldn't have changed a thing in the contract."

Gus's heart hammered in her chest. She'd pushed him too far for the second time in her role as leader of the vendors. And the results weren't any better this time around. He had a way of turning her sunshine to storm clouds faster than weather changed in the Midwest.

"Goodbye," she said.

Jack stalked to the door.

"You know," he said, "I really came here today to say thank-you."

And he was gone. One thing was certain. Jack was not an easy man to understand.

CHAPTER SIX

VIRGINIA HAMILTON PARKED Betty's red wagon in front of the Midway Bakery, where Gus stopped working, wiped her hands on her apron and leaned across the counter, smiling at her visitor.

"All ready for opening day?" Virginia asked.

"You tell me," Gus said. "How many customers do you think we'll have?"

"Depends on the weather, of course, and the local schools are still in session a few more weeks, but I'd say we can count on ten thousand or so. A lot of regulars come for opening day every year."

"Ten thousand cookies coming right up," Gus said, laughing. "The rest of the special cookie cutters I ordered should be in tomorrow. I think you've already seen the carousel horse, but wait till you see the roller coasters—especially the new Sea Devil—on a cookie. My favorite is the Starlight Point skyline. We plan to ice those cookies in dark twilight colors so the coaster lights will really pop."

Movement on the midway caught her attention. Jack Hamilton rode slowly past her shop on an old tandem bicycle, one of the employee loaners. The vacant seat made him look like a man dancing alone on an empty floor. He waved and continued down the midway, a rubber band around the leg of his suit pants.

Virginia waved to her son and turned back to Augusta. "I know you're busy, but can I borrow a minute to talk about my summer project? I'd like to get the plans going right away."

"What can I do?" Gus asked, striving for a neutral tone.

"I was thinking," Virginia said. "All these young men and women will probably be parents someday. Most of our older employees already are." She reached across the counter and laid her hand on Gus's arm. "Family is very important here at Starlight Point."

And they have no idea how lucky they are. Virginia had lost her husband, but she still had three children close at hand. As an only child with parents who moved often because of her father's job, Augusta craved the sense of family and belonging that everyone else seemed to have. But she did have her aunt and a fledgling business—otherwise she'd still be adrift.

"Of course," Gus said as she forced her thoughts back to Virginia's summer project. "It's a family amusement park, gotta love families. But what would you like me to do?"

This was getting scary. Was she supposed to teach them about family values? Natural childbirth? Installing a car seat correctly? Sibling rivalry?

Betty snored loudly in her wagon. She'd seen lots of summer improvement programs come and go. Maybe dog grooming had been one of them.

"What is an important thing that all parents should be able to do?" Virginia asked.

"Um…tie shoes? Sing the alphabet in two languages? Apply Band-Aids?"

"Make a birthday cake!" Virginia exclaimed. She smiled broadly and clapped her hands together once, leaving them joined.

"Oh," Gus said. "That was my next guess."

"Every parent should be able to bake and decorate a birthday cake for their child."

"I think so, too. But they can also get one from a bakery," Gus suggested, grinning. "I could recommend a good one for anyone looking."

"But not every year, dear. Moms and dads should bake a cake, frost it, make it look pretty and be able to write their child's name on it. And their age."

"I think most people figure it out," Gus said. "I learned how to make a birthday cake from my aunt."

"Unfair advantage. Not everyone has an aunt Augusta," Virginia said. "Some people never figure it out and they disappoint their kids every year." She dropped her large purse onto the counter and dug through it, finally pulling out a packet of wallet-sized photos in a yellowed cellophane holder.

"See this picture? This is Jack's fifth birthday."

Gus took the photo, which showed an adorable dark-haired and dark-eyed boy at a kitchen table. Disgracing the table in front of him was the ugliest birthday cake in the world. It was an uneven round shape, covered in lumpy chocolate frosting. *Canned frosting.* A squiggly red line—probably from the dreadful white tubes sold in grocery stores—made a crooked border. In the center, uncertain writing appeared to spell out *Happy Birthday, Jack* above a disproportionate and crooked number five. The only things that pulled the scene together were the five flaming candles and the happy family behind him.

His father, looking much like Jack did right now, held a girl who appeared to be about three. Virginia, much younger, had a hand on Jack's shoulder.

"That's our middle daughter, June," Virginia said. "She's in New York City working as a dancer in a Broadway production. Our younger daughter hadn't come along yet when that picture was taken."

"It's a beautiful picture," Gus said.

Virginia looked at her, both eyebrows raised.

Gus laughed. "Okay. All except for the cake."

They both laughed, and the sound echoed under the steel awning. Betty climbed out of the wagon. She licked her owner's hand and wagged her tail. Maybe she knew the word *cake* or she just liked a good party.

"See my point?" Virginia asked. "With your talent, you could improve the birthdays of hundreds, even thousands of children."

"That many? That's a lot of birthdays."

"We have two thousand employees here this summer."

Gus's shoulders sank. "You want me to teach two thousand people to make a fancy birthday cake?" Right now, all she could think of was baking enough cookies for one day—opening day, only seventy-two hours away.

Virginia took a long, slow breath. "Not all two thousand. Always made it a requirement in the past—didn't want people to miss out on a good thing. But this season is different. Life's too short to make people do things they don't want to do. Or have time for. So I'm making it voluntary this summer. My STRIPE program is getting soft in its old age—that'll shock some of our longtime employees, I know. People who want to learn to make a cake can do it." She shrugged. "The rest of them will miss out."

"I understand that the STRIPE clause is in the contracts," Gus said.

Virginia shrugged. "I'll take it out. My son, Jack, is officially taking over, but I'm still his mother and have some influence. Besides—" she paused and smiled "—I don't think anyone's going to fight me on making it voluntary."

"I still don't know," Gus said. She wasn't sure she could handle the STRIPE program, but her thoughts swung to Virginia's influence. Could she be an ally in contract negotiations?

Doubtful. Blood was thicker than water.

"You'll probably have only a couple hundred students at the most. And you'll have help. I always get volunteers."

"I'm just worried about spreading myself too thin, running these three bakeries while my aunt handles the downtown one."

In answer, Virginia held up the picture, raised her eyebrows and pointed to the ugly cake in front of her adorable son.

"Oh, all right," Gus said.

Birthdays tugged at her heart. They represented permanence, family and tradition. No matter what part of the country or world her father's job took their little family to, birthdays were celebrated the same. How could she pass up the chance to make hundreds or thousands of birthdays brighter?

Virginia squeezed Gus's arm. "I'll be your first student. Jack turns twenty-seven on June first, which is also my birthday. Best present I ever got. Maybe you could help me surprise him with a cake. My daughter June will be here that weekend and of course so will Evie. Think you could give her the day off?"

"Sure. She's going to be my account manager and supervise the Lake Breeze bakery, but family birthdays are more important. I'll help you learn to make a perfect cake, but only because I love a challenge."

Virginia laughed. "I need people like you and your aunt to cheer me up. This is my first summer without Ford in more than thirty years." She tried to cover her tears by leaning down to scratch under Betty's chin. "I wonder sometimes how all this can go on…but my Jack has a will of iron."

"I've heard that," Gus commented.

"But a soft heart," Virginia added. She picked up Betty, plunked her in the wagon and rolled away.

Gus wondered just how soft Jack's heart was.

TOSHA, BERNIE AND several other vendors came by as Gus finished stocking and cleaning the Midway Bakery. The sign crew had already been there and a large electric cookie with the name Aunt Augusta's Midway Bakery hung over the shop.

"I should get a new sign," Bernie said. "Had the same hand-painted French-fry sign for fifteen years."

"Can't afford it this year," Tosha commented.

Gus propped her elbows on her counter. "I'm sorry. I tried to see him before the deadline. Three times. I should've fought harder for all of you."

"Nonsense," Tosha said. "It's business. And you're not responsible for all of us. You've got enough on your plate. I plan to see how this summer goes and then reevaluate for next year. Gonna take it one ice-cream cone at a time."

"Summer hasn't even started and we're already in too deep to change anything," one of the souvenir vendors said. Ricardo sold Starlight Point hats, shirts, key chains and plastic snow globes featuring the roller coasters and the Star Spiral. "Got all my merchandise ordered already."

"One thing I'm not short on is employee applications," Tosha said.

"Me, too," Bernie agreed. "But I only need

a few summer workers. Had to turn a bunch of 'em away this year. Way more than usual."

"A friend in human resources told me Starlight Point was cutting the summer workforce ten percent across the board. That's two hundred people they're not hiring," Tosha said.

"Apparently the new management figures on keeping more of the profits for themselves," Ricardo grumbled. "I think they're going to learn some things the hard way."

"Doesn't solve the problem of our contracts," Hank reminded the group. "That's what I'm worried about right now."

"We could try renegotiating later in the summer," Gus suggested.

"Don't see why Jack would do that," Bernie said, "unless it was in his favor."

"I guess I don't, either," Gus admitted. "The only thing I can do right now is get all my shops ready for Saturday and hope like crazy I'll make so much money this summer I can cheerfully hand over a chunk of the profits."

They all nodded seriously.

"And if I don't, I'll chase him down and pelt him with rubber bands until he either cries uncle or names a roller coaster after me. The Zinger."

"That's the spirit," Tosha said. "Now back to work."

Gus headed for the Wonderful West and her Last Chance bakery. With her long stride, she zipped past her friends setting up their food and souvenir stands, power walked by the Scrambler and passed the old Silver Streak coaster that had stood by the bayside of the peninsula for forty years. Carousel music put a spring in her step and strengthened her hopes for a great season.

A bicycle bell jingled right behind her, cutting into "In the Good Old Summertime" tinkling from the carousel organ.

"Ride?" Jack asked.

He pulled in front of her on the red tandem bicycle. Although early in the summer, he already had a nice tan. His dark hair waved back from his forehead, his deep brown eyes less serious than usual.

Gus stopped on the bright white concrete, which was baking in the afternoon sun.

The ride was tempting. The Wonderful West was a good hike from the front entrance, and her hair was already stuck to the back of her neck. But the shade trees were just ahead. She could make a break for them and resist the charming and enigmatic Jack—the man who made her heart race and her blood boil.

"Depends on where you're going," she said in an attempt to stall and escape gracefully.

"Canada," he answered. "It's just across the lake."

"I figured. Are you a decent driver? How's your safety record on this thing?"

Jack planted both feet, balancing the bike between his long legs. Gus felt the heat even more. Why did the company owner and general enigma have to be so attractive?

"See this scar?" he asked, pointing at a small white line on his chin. "That was from my first bike accident."

"How old were you?"

"Twenty-five. I've gotten more careful since then."

"I see," she said. "I'm considering your risky offer."

"Last Chance."

"I'm thinking."

"No, I mean, I assume you're headed for your Last Chance bakery. You might as well get on and save your energy for opening day.

I'm hoping for fifteen thousand people. At least."

At the thought of baking fifteen thousand cookies, Gus surrendered and swung her leg over the seat in back. She would need all her energy if his prediction came true. From the backseat, her view was all broad shoulders and tailored suit. Why didn't he get heatstroke in those suits?

"I can't see anything from back here," she said.

"Don't need to. You can't steer, either."

Before she could protest, the bike started rolling. Gus gripped the handlebar and pedaled, trying to accustom herself to being totally at someone else's mercy. She focused on the shops, restaurants and trees whizzing by. She attempted to summon carefree childhood memories of racing on a bike, the wind in her hair. But she wasn't fooling anyone. She wanted to steer that bike like kids wanted to catch Santa on Christmas Eve.

Especially when Jack careened much too close to a tree. And when he skirted the edge of a curb in front of the HoneyBee kiddie coaster. He nearly crashed into an oncoming bike, but swept to the side at the last second and gave Gus only a brief glimpse of the near disaster.

The man was a maniac on a bike.

"I want off," she said.

"Trust me. I could do this with my eyes closed."

"I think you *are*."

He finally stopped in front of her Western-themed bakery sandwiched between the shooting gallery and the train tracks. She stepped off the bike, straightened her apron and admired her new sign as she tried to regain her equilibrium. The sign was like the one at the Midway Bakery, but *Aunt Augusta's Last Chance Bakery* was spelled out in neon ropes and the cookie wore a cowboy hat.

"Nice," Jack commented. "You're breathing new life into these bakeries."

He planted his feet again. Gus thought for a moment he'd put down the kickstand and invite himself in. Instead he sat and looked at her as if he were at a loss. He must have a million things to do with only days until the season started. Just like she did.

"Work to do," she said, unable to restrain a smile.

He nodded. “Want me to pick you up later? It gets pretty lonely on this bike by myself.”

“I think I’ll take the train,” she said, sounding much more flirtatious than she wanted to.

“Too dangerous. We’re training new engineers before the season starts.”

Gus laughed and then sobered quickly, thinking of how late she’d be here tonight and how she’d have to struggle all summer to make a profit. She’d be baking and decorating faster than the spinning rides in Kiddieland.

Gus couldn’t invite any kind of a friendship with Jack Hamilton—too many people depended on her commitment and hard work. And her current loyalty was to the other vendors. Even after only a few weeks, they were starting to feel like family.

“You’re a busy man, I hear. Too busy to be bothered with lease vendors like me.”

The smile creasing his face and lighting his eyes flashed out like a switched-off bulb. Gus felt a stab of guilt at her bitter words. But they were the truth.

She walked away and shoved through the swinging saloon-style doors into her bakery.

CHAPTER SEVEN

JACK'S GUT WAS doing somersaults as he did a walk-through of Starlight Point on the afternoon before opening day. If he'd had to sign anything right now, he wouldn't have been able to hold the pen steady. The nervous tension was like a vibrating drum in his chest, its rhythms spiking upward through his neck and shoulders.

He had done this final walk-through with his father every year of his life. He barely remembered the early years, but he had seen pictures—him riding in a red wagon behind his father as he pointed out all the changes and new rides constructed over the winter. He noticed everything—even as a child—any new sign, a different paint color on the trim of a building, a cart parked in a new location. And the rides, of course he noticed those. He was still a ride junkie after all these years.

But he was all grown up. His mother hauled Betty around in that red wagon now.

"Want company?" Evie asked, her voice and her hand on his arm equally soft. His youngest sister had always been a quiet force in an energetic house. June had tended toward fiery competition mixed with fierce love and loyalty. Evie was more like their mother. Quietly determined, strong underneath.

"I'd love your company," Jack said. "But…"

"Don't worry." Evie grinned, pointing at her running shoes. "I'll keep up."

"Good thing. Or you're going in the wagon."

They walked briskly, both of them blessed with the long Hamilton legs. From the front entrance to the farthest Western-themed train station at the tip of the peninsula, it was just shy of one and a half miles. Starlight Point was a deep peninsula jutting into the lake, covered with rides, food, noise and people. A long beach on the lakeside and a curved marina on the bay side made sure the fun didn't end where the water began.

"Are we going through the hotel, too, floor by floor and hall by hall?" Evie asked.

"That's your favorite part. When you were little and got to come along, you used to make up stories about all the famous people you imagined staying in the rooms and walking the hallways."

"In pretty dresses and fancy dinner clothes."

Jack grimaced. "If you must."

"Just don't hide then jump out and scare me. I hate that."

"Come on," Jack said. "I haven't done that since…"

"Last year."

"Has it been that long? I've got some catching up to do. People will think I've lost my reckless charm."

Evie was silent a moment as they passed through a park entrance toward the beach. They clunked through the turnstile and paused to watch the water as they leaned on the ornate iron beach railing.

Jack turned and found his little sister staring at him. "What?" he asked.

"I was thinking how much you look like Dad."

"Not sure that's a compliment. Do I look that old?"

"No," she said. "Not yet anyway. Maybe after a few months in charge of this place."

Jack laughed and draped a long arm over Evie's shoulders. She was only twenty-one, and the six years between them made him feel protective of her, made him wonder how and when he was going to tell her the truth about their father's debt. He couldn't put it off forever and risk dumping a mess on his family. Like his father had.

"I miss him, too," he said. "I wish I could go back in time and say some things. Ask some things. If I'd had any idea..."

Evie wiped a tear from her cheek, pulling back to look at her brother. "If you'd known you'd be running Starlight Point this summer, what would you have asked Dad?"

"How to do *every*thing."

"You already know everything about Starlight Point. You've been training to run it since you were born. I thought Dad shared everything with you already?"

Jack frowned and stared at his feet.

"You've been his right-hand man," Evie insisted.

Jack turned his gaze to the water, not sure how much to reveal to his younger sister. Protecting her meant lying to her.

"You know," Evie continued, "the secret trapdoors, the key to the safe, how to get gum off the midway, what we do with the giant collection of coins we find under the coasters. All that stuff."

"I know about the coins at least. We donate that money to a local charity. Mom picks one every year."

"See," Evie said, smiling and patting his arm. "You'll be fine."

"I wish I had as much confidence in me as you do." He tried to keep his voice light as he took her arm and steered them down the boardwalk toward the hotel.

After his father's unexpected death, his mother had turned the company over to her three children. They were equal partners and owners. His sisters had unanimously elected Jack the leader and president because June lived out of state and Evie had one year of college left. Jack's excitement about the leader's job hadn't lasted long, but his mother and sisters believed in him. And he had no choice but to keep moving forward.

"I'm a third-owner now," Evie said, "and I'd like to enjoy this last day before all mayhem cuts loose."

THE HOTEL BAKESHOP looked like a cookie blizzard had swept in, burying it in stacks of carefully wrapped summer-themed cookies.

"Good!" Gus exclaimed when Evie stepped through the door. "You're here. I'm desperate for organization and someone with brains and sanity."

Jack appeared right behind his sister. He ruffled Evie's hair. "Then I guess I'm your man," he said.

"What's the matter?" Evie asked. "You look frazzled."

Although Gus's apron was covered in hearts, she didn't feel very warm and fuzzy. Warm maybe, but only because it was hotter than heck in the small bakery with the oven blazing. She had dozens of cookies left to bake, a temperamental new oven in the Last Chance and about twenty summer employees whose decorating skills were—to put it kindly—like a kindergartner's.

Gus wanted to unload on Evie and confide all her worries. In only a week of working side by side, Gus had found Evie to be a great listener, incredibly practical and someone she'd like to befriend. She could use a friend.

But she forced herself to remember that

Evie was a Hamilton. And Gus was not saying a word in front of Jack. She wouldn't show weakness. Wouldn't flinch. She would put on a brave face for herself and all the vendors, who, ironically, considered making a huge summer profit an act of defiance. Even though she was his sister and technically an owner, none of the vendors considered Evie to be in the enemy camp. Perhaps because she was so nice, and word had got around that Jack was running the show, not his sisters. His name was on the contracts, not Evie's and June's.

Gus picked up a cookie shaped like the Silver Streak coaster. She'd decorated it for her helpers to use as an example. It was covered with smooth silver-and-white icing with little colored dots representing riders in a coaster train. Just for fun, she waved it under Jack's nose before holding it up.

"See this cookie?" Gus said, forgetting to answer Evie's question. "I'm going to sell so many of these I'll need a dump truck to haul out all the cash."

Gus couldn't quite meet Jack's eyes. She wanted to run herself through the mixer every time she thought about how she was attracted to him. She wanted to run him through the blender every time he opened his mouth and mentioned business.

"Reserving twenty out of every one hundred trucks for you, of course," she said. She directed her words at Jack even though she knew Evie would profit, as well. Why Evie wanted to spend her summer slaving over books for a vendor was beyond Gus, but she was grateful to have her help.

Perhaps people wondered why Aunt Augusta was working long shifts at her niece's bakery when she could be taking bus tours with old gals her age. Gus didn't want to admit how desperately she needed her aunt's help. *Maybe there's a lot people don't know about the Hamiltons, too.*

Right now, Gus knew she wanted Jack to get back to work and out from under her skin.

"Jack and I are doing our final walk-through," Evie said, breaking the awkward silence. "We do this every year on the day before the season opening."

"Just to check everything out?"

"And enjoy having the place to ourselves

one more time before thousands of people start showing up every day."

"Lucky for you," Gus said, "they do show up."

"Of course," Jack said. "But this is the last chance for it to feel like our own family's park."

"Gotcha," Gus said. "Maybe I should enjoy the cozy family feel of my bakery here before people have the nerve to come in and buy cookies."

Gus sighed and bit her lip. Despite her exhaustion, frustration and need for caffeine, she handed the Silver Streak cookie to Jack. It was better than an olive branch on the eve of the big battle.

"Good luck with your walk-through," she said. "If you happen to know anything about electrical controllers, you can stop in my bakery in the Wonderful West and see why that oven won't hold a consistent temperature. Until it does, I'm doing double baking right here."

Evie stepped forward. "Want me to stay and help? I've been having fun learning to bake this past week. I may even give up accounting. Jack can handle the walk-through by himself."

Gus smiled at Evie. "Appreciate your offer, but I've got some help coming in. Lucky for me, my aunt doesn't have plans on a Friday night, and a few of my experienced employees from my downtown shop are coming over to bail me out. Until I get more decorators and bakers trained here, I'm going to be icing cookies in my sleep."

"I'll stop by later to check on you," Evie said. "And my offer of decorating cookies still stands." She shoved her brother toward the door.

Jack glanced over his shoulder with an unreadable expression.

GUS FIRST REALIZED something was wrong by a sudden silence. It lasted only ten seconds and was followed by swearing. Voluminous swearing. The cursing of a man who'd been around other top-notch colorful-language users his whole life. She pulled out the done batch of cookies, laid the trays gently on the long marble counter and hustled to the front door of her bakeshop.

The Lake Breeze Hotel had been built long

before the peninsula was invaded by an amusement park. It had a large, old-fashioned lobby with polished hardwood floors, ornate stained-glass windows and an interior balcony. A long check-in counter covered one side of the lobby, across from a string of retail shops featuring toiletries and resort wear. A pancake restaurant took up one of the shorter sides, opposite a souvenir stand and the bakeshop owned by Gus.

All afternoon, she'd heard the one-hundred-year-old building coming to life for another season. Creaking, groaning, water rushing through pipes. Old hotel sounds mixed with the clang of tourist season made a music all its own. Gus heard it, but ignored it. She was putting her new oven to the test, running batch after batch of cookies through it. Sea Devil, Silver Streak, carousel and cookies in a dozen other shapes familiar to Starlight Point guests had come and gone through the oven four dozen at a time. At the end of the day tomorrow, Gus would know whether she'd gone overboard or barely made a ripple.

But now, she stood transfixed in the door of her bakery.

What she saw made her want to grab her cookies and run. Water. Streams of water making their way across the lobby, spewing and gushing from a wall on the opposite side. A wave slid over the gleaming floors, getting closer and closer to her door.

"Shut off the main!" a man yelled. "The main!"

If Gus had known what the main was or where it was, she would've been all over it. Instead, she bolted into her shop and grabbed anything, everything that was on or near the floor. Chairs up on tables, electrical cords unplugged. Flour in bags anywhere near the floor, sugar, cellophane cookie bags, boxes of finished cookies. Everything. She stretched, reached, hauled and lifted until every high surface in her bakeshop was covered with the refugees from lower down.

The shouting in the lobby amplified now. Male voices, angry. Maybe it was a good thing Aunt Augusta hadn't gotten there yet. She'd either be out there yelling, too, just for the heck of it, or telling them all to watch their language. She never knew with Aunt Augusta. Radios squawked with information and orders.

She risked a look. The water was only inches away from her front door, but it appeared to have stalled. Maybe this old hotel wasn't level and the crooked foundation was slightly in her favor. Or maybe someone shut off the main somewhere. She'd take whatever she could get.

Maintenance men, supervisors, bellboys in training and housekeepers trudged through the water, some of it ankle deep. Someone had opened the door leading to the beach and water gushed through it. So the hotel was slanted toward the beach. Good to know. Gus was never so happy to be on the opposite end of the lobby. One of the desk clerks used a broom to sweep water toward the open beach door. A bellboy appeared with another broom and they went at it like an Olympic curling team, sweeping and guiding the water off the century-old floor.

This was a disaster. Upholstered lobby chairs were wet up to their seats, the carpet in the retail shops and anything stored near or on the floor was wrecked. Who knew what shape the pancake shop was in. Judging from the congregation of maintenance men, she had a feeling the water-main break must be in the corner where the pancake restaurant met the hallway leading to the guest parking lot.

Gus took off her shoes. She wore shorts and a T-shirt under her apron, so her clothes would stay dry. Unlike the maintenance guys across the lobby. She wished she had spare towels to take them, but they looked too ticked off to care that they were wet. Grabbing a broom from the back room of her bakery, Gus joined the sweeping team in the lobby. She couldn't even think about how this was going to affect the hotel guests arriving tomorrow. Right now, the water had to go somewhere, and she wanted it off the lobby floor and as far from her shop as it could go.

Sweep, shove, push, repeat. Five people were sweeping now, but the water managed to slip back between them if they slowed down for a moment. Gus had a strong back and shoulders, but she'd worked twelve-hour days baking, decorating, cleaning and stocking all week. She would have to risk her liver later by combining painkillers and a glass of wine to ease her into a night's sleep. She was going to need it.

From the corner of her eye, she saw him arrive. She didn't even need to look. Few people were as tall as Jack Hamilton. Gus was on the end of the sweeping string closest to the maintenance men. They were looking at a pipe going up the corner of the lobby. It was almost as big around as Gus's waist. If Jack wanted to know what was going on, he'd be coming right past her.

Curious, Gus maneuvered closer to the corner with her broom and continued sweeping, making sure to get every ounce of water headed the right direction. Jack paused next to her, his eyes washing over her bare legs and feet, but his expression unchanging. He stalked up to the men around the pipe.

"What the heck happened?" Jack asked.

"Standpipe broke."

"Crap."

"No kidding," a man with a large wrench said. "We were testing the sprinkler system. Fire inspector will be in this afternoon to sign off for occupancy."

"Any idea why the pipe failed?" Jack asked.

"Must've cracked over the winter. We drain the whole hotel, but if any water gets left in the pipes and freezes...well, it's an old pipe. Mighta just broke."

Jack stripped off his suit jacket and looked around for somewhere to set it down. The chairs had all been shoved back, and the floor was wet. He looked so exasperated Gus felt sorry for him.

"I'll put that in my shop," she said. "It's dry in there."

He handed her the coat wordlessly, his glance lingering on her for a second, and then he turned back to the maintenance guys.

"Is this a major job?" Gus heard him ask as she headed across the lobby. She didn't catch the answer, but she heard Jack's muttered cursing in response.

Gus decided she'd be better off decorating the cooled cookies in her bakery. Other workers had already begun to arrive to help with the damage cleanup. She might never see her broom again, but that was peanuts compared to Jack's problems.

CHAPTER EIGHT

JACK WONDERED WHY something couldn't go right. His father had made it all look effortless. Of course, as Jack had recently discovered, in addition to bottling up his anxiety until his heart gave out, Ford Hamilton had been a master at concealing his problems. Looking around at the soggy hotel lobby filled with wet and tired employees, Jack knew there was no hiding this problem. The only thing coaxing half a smile out of him was Mel Preston striding across the wet floor much too quickly.

"Watch it!" Jack yelled.

His warning was too late. Mel skidded out of control, flailed his arms wildly and fell on his can. He groaned and lay totally still. "Am I dead?" he asked.

There was total silence for a full two seconds, then uproarious laughter from the assembled cleanup and maintenance crew. Jack, still chuckling, extended a hand and helped his best friend up.

"Thanks," Mel said.

"Thank *you*. We needed a laugh. And there's nothing funny about this mess."

"Heard about it over the radio. Standpipe, huh?"

Jack nodded. "I thought the yearly fire inspections were done a week ago, but apparently not. We've been preoccupied with the new ride so much..." He met his friend's eyes. "I guess it's not so much *we* as it is *I*. Juggling everything and making it all ready for opening day—seems I've got a few things to learn."

"Building maintenance guys ought to have handled this. Not your fault. I wonder why the pipe broke."

"Maybe not fully emptied for the winter, maybe it was just old. That's what they tell me."

"Either way, timing is awful. Are guests scheduled to stay here tomorrow?"

"Yep."

Mel used his thumb and ring finger to squeeze his temples, wrinkling the skin on his forehead. "You're not thinking of getting this cleaned up and ready on time, are you? You're nuts, but not *that* nuts."

"New pipe's on its way, we're bringing in big fans to dry the carpet, and I've got a cleaning crew on overtime."

"What about the fire inspection? Can't open the hotel without that."

"Already talked to the fire chief. He says we can open if we keep a truck and two firefighters on the premises twenty-four hours a day."

"And you're planning to do that?"

"At least for the weekend until we can get the system back up and pass inspection."

"I don't want to step on your big ugly toes or anything, but are you sure you have the manpower to tie up two guys and a truck all day and night?" Mel asked.

Jack unrolled and wrung out his shirtsleeves then rolled them back up.

"I heard our seasonal staff might be cut some this year is all," Mel said. "Maybe I heard wrong."

"You heard right," Jack said, avoiding eye contact.

"None of my business, just asking if you have the emergency responders you need to cover a big opening day with some of them babysitting this old place."

"It sounds like a pain in the neck, but it's still better than refunding money or finding someplace else to stay for the two hundred and fifty guests coming in tomorrow." Jack draped an arm around his friend's shoulders and muscled him across the lobby away from the maintenance and cleaning crew. "And I don't want to start the season with a failure on the books. Bad press is not the way for me to begin my career in charge," he said quietly.

Mel nodded. He was the only person, aside from his family, Jack would admit that to. There were a whole lot of other things he ought to tell his family and Mel, but now was not the time.

"Guess I'll pitch in, too," Mel said.

"Thanks. Want to start by helping me unload the fans?" He inclined his head toward the parking-lot entrance. "I hear the truck backing up right now."

EVENING DARKENED THE antique lobby windows. Jack's suit jacket was gone, carried away by Gus hours ago. The sleeves of his white dress shirt were rolled up over his elbows and his shirttail hung out one side. He'd shoved his tie into the back pocket of his pants. His black leather dress shoes—his favorites because they were comfortable enough to endure miles of Starlight Point walking—were wrecked like a wedding dress in a washing machine. The legs of his pants were wet halfway up his calves.

Hauling in the fans had been only the beginning. He and the overtime crew had sorted ruined merchandise in the lobby retail shops and loaded what could be saved onto a truck to be figured out later. They'd set up fans to dry the carpeting and moved on to the next shop. By the time they'd gotten to the pancake restaurant, they were already dirty and exhausted.

His rumbling stomach finally reminded Jack that he'd skipped lunch and worked through dinner. He suspected many of his employees had also missed dinner and were probably going on twelve hours of solid work. It was tempting to throw in the towel.

If the hotel didn't open tomorrow, they'd have to find other lodging for all the inconvenienced guests and offer comp packages. It would also be really bad business, and people wouldn't be so likely to come back. But he was starving and tired.

Jack hauled a soggy box of paper take-out cartons from under a counter in the pancake shop. He dropped them on the cart destined for the Dumpster. As he straightened, rubbing his aching back, a tray of cookies appeared in front of him.

The full force of Gus's beauty hit him as she was illuminated in the emergency lighting. Maybe it was the aroma coming off the cookies. Maybe it was the wide smile she wore. A sympathetic smile that shot right to his heart.

"You must be starving. Evie told me you didn't have lunch or dinner."

He shook his head, not trusting himself to say anything without screwing up.

"I know cookies are no substitute, but give it a try," she said. "I've got fresh bread in the oven and I sent one of my helpers out for turkey and ham. We'll have sandwiches ready for the cleanup and maintenance crews in about a half hour."

Jack stared speechlessly, amazed and grateful.

"Consider this an appetizer," she said. "Which one would you like?"

Jack finally looked at the cookies. Small replicas of the rides and attractions at Starlight Point covered the tray. The newest ride, the Sea Devil, cozied up to the oldest coaster, the Silver Streak. The Lake Breeze Hotel, the Star Spiral, even the skyline at night were represented in sugar and dough.

"Can I pick more than one?" he asked.

"You can have them all," Gus said, laughing. "I must have eighty dozen cookies ready to go for my three shops."

"I hope you sell them all tomorrow," he said. "On top of good sales for you, it's great advertising for us."

Jack picked up the Lake Breeze Hotel cookie and bit the roof off. He closed his eyes. "Heavenly. It takes me back to the night I met you."

"A whopping two weeks ago."

When she laughed, her eyes sparkled. Her skin flushed, bringing pink tinges to her creamy milk complexion. He wanted to pull her into his arms and kiss her until all his problems disappeared.

"I'm curious," she said.

Jack snapped back to attention. He wondered if his thoughts showed on his face.

"Which one is your favorite?" she asked.

He finished off the hotel cookie, the wonderful feeling of sugar rushing through his veins and—temporarily at least—clearing his head.

"The night skyline."

He picked up the cookie, looking at it closely. It had a straight bottom and a gently curving top side. Dark blue icing—the color of the night sky before it got completely dark—contrasted with the white lines and dots representing the lights on the coasters and tall rides that had created a sparkling skyline every night of his life. All winter long, those lights gave him a dose of hope and excitement about the summer that was always coming.

"Why?" Her voice was soft, almost a caress.

"It reminds me of something I will never forget. Something good."

He swore he saw the hint of tears in her eyes, but he couldn't imagine what he had said to upset her this time.

"Me—"

"Hey! Cookies. Whew, I'm starving." Mel Preston shoulder-checked Jack and grabbed two cookies off the tray. "Thought you were going to hog them all for a minute there."

Gus gave Mel a mock-serious look. "You should wash your hands before eating," she said.

"Beautiful lady, I've eaten so much dirt in the ten years I've worked here, I've probably got an acre of garden growing somewhere inside." He pointed to his abs when he spoke.

"Augusta Murphy, this is my chief of maintenance, Mel Preston," Jack said.

"I'd shake your hand, but you might have noticed how revoltingly filthy I am."

"Nice to meet you. And I think I owe you. One of my employees called me a little while ago and said a maintenance man named Mel had fixed our fussy oven at the Last Chance earlier today. Thank you. I was getting desperate."

"Boss sent me over there."

"Your boss?"

"Jack."

Gus turned to Jack. "I should thank you, too."

"Always liked electrical controllers," Mel continued, wolfing down cookies. "Went to school to be an electrician, but I don't always do that kind of work here."

"What do you usually do?"

"Whatever the big guy says."

"Sounds like a smart decision," she said.

"I'll be out with sandwiches later. I'm assuming we're in for a long night."

"We are," Jack said. "But you're under no obligation to stay. It's not your problem."

Gus drew her eyebrows together and gave Jack a look somewhere between confused and hurt.

"Not my problem?" she asked.

"Well, no. It's nice of you to help… I appreciate it…but—" He wanted to say that Starlight Point was *his* problem, *his* responsibility. If anyone was going to be wet, tired, hungry and desperate, it should be *him.* He should be the one getting no sleep on the night before the season opening, not the woman in front of him who'd provided the only sweet spot in his day so far.

"Because I'm just a vendor?" she asked.

What? Where did that come from? She was new this year, so maybe she didn't know that the lease vendors were practically part of the family.

Or they had been until desperation made him alienate them.

"That's not what I meant," he said.

"And I'm not staying because it's an obligation," she said, her tone walking the line between hot and cold. "Neither are my employees, including your sister, who is serving cookies right now."

She spun around and headed for a group of maintenance men with her tray of cookies.

"Looking forward to those sandwiches," Mel called after her.

Mel eyed Jack with a curious expression. "Sometimes I'm a little late to the party when it comes to matters of the…um…heart and all—at least that's what my ex-wife says—but I think she likes you."

"What makes you think that?"

"She was totally immune to my charms, didn't you notice? The only explanation I can think of is that you got here first. And you're taller. That always helps."

"Our relationship is strictly business," Jack said.

"Sure," Mel answered. He finished off the two cookies in his hand with only two bites each. "Good thing, otherwise you really screwed up."

IT HAD TO be midnight. It might as well be midnight. Total darkness outside the hotel and total exhaustion between Augusta's shoulder blades. And tomorrow was opening day. At least guests wouldn't arrive until ten o'clock. If she hurried home and got right in bed, she might get enough sleep to ensure her survival of the big season opener. And all the days after that? She'd have to figure it out as she went.

The Lake Breeze Hotel was on the beach at the opposite end of the peninsula from the front parking lot. More than a mile of walking awaited her. The breeze was cool, ruffling her long dark hair. Maybe a walk would relax the tension out of her muscles and help her get to sleep faster.

Only a few lights dotted the midway. Tomorrow night, it would be ablaze while guests enjoyed the rides and games. Tonight was like Christmas Eve. Dark, but with the hush of anticipation and readiness. She walked quickly, shivering a little, anxious for her warm bed.

Gus nearly jumped out of her skin when an engine sounded behind her and a headlight bounced up and down, unevenly illuminating the path in front of her. She stepped quickly to the side, afraid she'd be run down and killed, leaving her many employees adrift. Her aunt Augusta would be alone. Again.

The cart jerked to a stop. Of course. Jack Hamilton. He put the parking brake on, killed the engine and doused the headlight. Jack got out of the cart and faced her in the darkness, blocking her path. His movements were surprisingly strong and deliberate for someone as tired as he had to be. In the darkness of the amusement park midway, it was easy to see him not as her enigmatic and unpredictable employer, but as a man. A man who wore a wet suit and kayaked, a man who stole cookies, a man in a bedraggled suit who'd just put in at least an eighteen-hour day. A man whose dark hair waved away from his face and whose eyes made her want to know the thoughts behind them.

"I heard you left the hotel a few minutes ago," he said.

He was asking about her?

"Evie told me," he continued. "I kept an eye out for you, wanted to catch you."

He was watching for her? Gus couldn't decide if that was incredibly sweet or a little spooky.

"I wanted to give you a ride up front," he said. Even in the darkness, she could see his teeth flash in a smile.

"You don't have to do that."

"Yes, I do. You didn't have to stay this late."

"A simple thank-you would do."

"Thank you."

Without a word, he pulled her against him, his arms strong but tender. Gus was stunned. Jack Hamilton was hugging her? That was definitely his cheek resting against hers, a long day's worth of stubble grazing her skin. His scent was all around her, the smell of warm skin in the cool air, a hint of musty water from the hotel pipes. Something about it was perfect and summed up Jack Hamilton to her. As frustrating as he could be, he had this place in his blood.

What was she doing, letting him hold her this long? This was beyond a friendly thank-you hug. Because it was so late and she was so tired, the sensation was magnified. They were alone on the silent midway. She slipped her arms around his waist, wanting to push him away for being such a jerk, but drawing him closer instead. When was the last time she'd been in a man's arms like this? It had been too long.

She would back away in ten seconds, she told herself. Only ten seconds more of this feeling or she'd completely forget what side of the fence she was supposed to be on. She tried reminding herself that this man's stubbornness was costing her thirty thousand bucks. But his touch felt like a million dollars.

Fifteen seconds went by. Or twenty. It was hard to keep track. Her feelings were like the cotton candy they sold in bags on the midway. Delicious but delicate. They would melt away in a second.

Gus released him and stepped back, pushing him away with light fingers.

"What are you doing, Jack?"

"Unless I'm dreaming, that was a hug. And it was the best part of my day."

"We can't," she said.

"We were."

She held her hand up in a stop-the-car gesture. "This was a mistake. It's late. We're both giddy and tired."

"Didn't feel like a mistake to me," Jack said.

"Hugging the boss is a mistake for *me*. Tomorrow morning you're the man who owns all this and I'm just a vendor for the summer."

"So?"

She cocked her head to the side and raised

an eyebrow. "Maybe you didn't notice, but vendors aren't exactly in the first-class cabins on your ship."

Jack blew out a long exasperated breath. "Think it's so great owning all this? Tell you what. I'll trade you."

Gus laughed. "No, you wouldn't. You love this place. You eat, drink and breathe Starlight Point. You even smell like Starlight Point."

Jack gave her a funny look and turned away, facing the long midway ahead of them. His broad back was like a wall in front of her, only the chasing strobes on the coasters visible over his tall frame, his white shirt like a sail on a vast ocean. He stood still for so long she thought he almost forgot she was there.

"I'd do anything to save Starlight Point," he said quietly.

"Save it?" Did Starlight Point need to be rescued? It probably would if Jack continued to treat people like her and Tosha and Bernie the way he had.

Without answering, Jack got in the driver's seat. "I'll take you to your van," he said, not looking at her.

She hesitated.

"Don't worry. I'll keep my hands on the steering wheel."

It was almost disappointing, knowing she'd shoved him far enough to preserve whatever working relationship they had. She'd walked away from the delicious feeling of his arms around her. Permanently. She doubted he would ever do that again.

"I've seen your driving," she said, her tone light in an attempt to chase away the darkness between them. "Keeping your hands on the wheel won't help."

Jack exhaled loudly through his nose and waited.

Should she get into the cart with a man who ignited her senses but made her want to run for the fire hose? Or add a mile-long walk to a day that had already been a roller coaster? She glanced at the sky, every star reminding her how late it was. She got in the cart.

"I'm parked in the Star Spiral lot."

"I know."

"Spying on me?" she asked.

"You drive a huge pink van with a wedding cake on it."

Gus shrugged. "I'm sure I'm not the only one," she muttered.

Jack switched on the headlights and slowly drove along the midway. She wanted to ask if the cart went any faster, but the silence was safer. Jack hadn't said a word since the cart started moving. What would have happened if he'd kissed her? Would she have let him? It was useless to think of it. They'd both be better off forgetting it. For all she knew, Jack already had regrets.

Jack waved at the security guard in the booth as they drove through the front gate. Her pink van wasn't hard to spot in the empty parking lot.

When he parked the cart, Jack grabbed Gus's hand before she could step out. His other hand slipped to her elbow, gentle pressure insisting she stay for a minute.

"Thank you for everything you did tonight."

She swayed toward him, the darkness and exhaustion taking down her defenses.

"Just trying to help," she said. "I can't fix pipes, so food is my way of helping."

"Much appreciated. You have no idea how much."

She couldn't see his face in the dark, but she could guess what she'd find. Lines of pure exhaustion. Probably the same ones she wore. And tomorrow was the beginning of a one-hundred-day marathon. Time to call it a night.

Almost. She pulled her hand from his and climbed out of the cart, standing just out of his reach.

"Do you think you'll get the hotel ready for occupancy tomorrow?"

"Barely. If we're lucky. I'm headed back there now, got the midnight crew coming in. They'll be fresh and ready to go."

"And you?"

"I'm not so fresh—apparently I *smell* like Starlight Point—but I have to be there. I own the place."

Gus glanced over his head at the lights on the rides and the coasters. Her breath caught when she realized exactly where she was standing—in the parking lot, right outside the front gates. It was the view she loved. Her view.

She'd been five years old. Her parents had finally decided she was big enough to go on some of the rides and they'd come across the bay for an outing. Aunt Augusta was with them. It was a long day, a wonderful day.

When the park closed, her father had had to carry her out, half-asleep in his arms.

They'd been parked only a few rows from where she now stood. She remembered looking back at Starlight Point, the white lights on the rides, the twirling lights on the midway carousel just visible through the front gate, the tall lights chasing along the roller coasters. Everything was lit up against a sky the color of her favorite crayon in the box: midnight blue. She knew she would never forget the way she felt in that moment.

It was the image of Starlight Point she'd carried with her for twenty years. The memory hit her with such force she was glad her face wasn't visible in the darkness. She swiped at her cheeks.

Jack's family had given her that happy day and perpetually joyful memory, but she was all grown up now. She had a business to run, a loan to pay, employees who counted on her. Surrendering to a foolish attraction was not the way to begin the season.

"I should go," she said. "Long day tomorrow."

"Actually," Jack said, "it's just past midnight. Opening day is today."

"Happy opening day, Jack."

He said nothing, staring at the park instead. He didn't look like a man who owned an amusement park. That man should be colorfully dressed with a noisemaker in his pocket, a fake handlebar mustache and a hand buzzer for surprises. Jack was dark, somber. Instead of sitting on top of the world, he had the world on his shoulders.

"When you said 'save Starlight Point...'" she began.

Jack didn't answer; instead he turned the key and let the loud, rattling engine fill the silence.

Gus gave up, got in her van and pulled out of the narrow parking space. She risked a glance at Jack. He was still in the cart where she'd left him. He owned the place, yet he sat by himself wearing a ruined shirt in a dirty maintenance cart in the parking lot. It was hard to tell in the dark, but she was sure he was looking at the night skyline of Starlight Point.

Now that she knew the feel of his arms around her, she had no idea how she was going to resist him all summer.

CHAPTER NINE

A THUNDERSTORM JOLTED Jack out of bed at six in the morning. He'd gotten to sleep around three after finally seeing the Lake Breeze project to an end. For now. The fire inspectors would come on Monday, and until then, he had a crew standing by. One pumper, two firefighters. One more expense.

Autumn was a long way off, but Jack was already thinking of how he would address the pipes. He'd have a crew go through and update all of them. His sisters had always been after their father to restore and renovate the entire hotel, but Ford Hamilton had pursued a different plan—build bigger and better rides to draw larger crowds. Jack wondered if his sisters had a point. Make it more enticing for people to stay right there on the peninsula, and their dollars would stay with them.

That was a problem for another day. Right now, streaks of lightning cut the early-morning sky and crackled over the Star Spiral and the rest of the skyline.

Jack saw it all from his modest home on the Old Road. A small strip of land connecting the mainland to the peninsula, the Old Road had been the only way to Starlight Point. But storms and washouts had convinced the city to build the Point Bridge decades ago. Now houses like Jack's and his parents' a few doors down were considered an exclusive place to live, with access to the lake, the bay and Starlight Point.

Jack started the coffeepot and flipped on the television. He was almost afraid to see the weather report. He searched for the local news channel and saw his own face.

"Starlight Point opens for the season today," the newscaster said, "under the leadership of the next generation. Jack Hamilton will take over daily operations, replacing his father, Ford Hamilton, who died unexpectedly earlier this spring."

They rolled some film footage of maintenance crews working on the new ride about a week ago.

Jack grimaced as he watched himself on television looking confident and saying, "We're excited to add the Sea Devil to our list of world-class coasters." More PR shots followed, showing painting and other prep work. He caught a glimpse of a pink van on the midway in one of the camera angles. He wondered if Gus was awake. Was she watching the news and thinking about him, about last night?

He would see her today. Probably every day. Starlight Point was big, but not that big.

The weather report jerked his attention back to the television. "The storm is moving off across the lake and the weather should clear by midmorning. Great news for folks headed to the Point."

Jack took his coffee to the table on his covered deck. From there, he looked over Starlight Point. He wore only loose pajama bottoms, and the cool morning breeze raised gooseflesh on his bare chest. But the air was fresh. The rainstorm had washed the air, leaving a new spring smell in its wake. New beginnings, he thought, watching the seagulls flock in groups in the empty parking lot. A fresh start. If only it were that easy.

GUS MOVED SEVERAL containers of cookies from the back of the shop to the front counter while her summer employee Liz waited on customers. It would have been easier to carry the boxes without the cell phone crammed between her shoulder and ear, but Aunt Augusta was in a jam.

"I don't see it," the older lady said in Gus's ear. "I looked all over your desk."

"It's a black daily planner. Should be in the top drawer."

"Oh. You didn't say it was in a drawer."

Gus sighed, walked out the back door and sat on an old picnic table shaded by the building. The employee break area was concealed from guests and hemmed in by food and game stands all around. She could still hear the carousel music from the midway even though her aunt was making a racket ransacking the desk in her office at the Downtown Bakery. Gus propped an elbow on the table, leaned her head on her hand and closed her eyes.

"Find it?" she asked.

On the other end of the line, Aunt Augusta hooted triumphantly.

"Good. Now flip to November. I know I have several weddings penciled in already, but I can't remember the dates."

Gus listened to her aunt flipping pages. It was midafternoon on opening day and she was already wondering why on earth she'd thought she could run four bakeshops at the same time. She felt like a swimmer desperately treading water and longing for the shore. For most of her life, Gus had searched for solid ground. Moving as much as her family had, there was only one place she ever thought of as home. And she was there right now.

Aunt Augusta's home in Bayside was the one place of permanence in her life, and by moving here, Gus had finally found where she belonged. She hoped. Keeping it all afloat didn't look possible right now, but failure was not an option. There was no place else for her to go. Her aunt had assured her that, although pushing sixty years old, she was up to the challenge of managing daily operations at the Bayside shop. Right now, it didn't sound that way.

"Okay. I'm on the November page. Let me get my glasses." There was a long pause and some crackling sounds as her aunt put down the phone and then picked it up again. "You wrote in the first two Saturdays and the number of servings. Two hundred fifty and five hundred."

"That second wedding is a big one." She felt the table jiggle with the weight of someone sitting across from her, but she didn't look. Her eyes needed a longer break and she wanted to focus on her conversation.

"Tell you what, Aunt Augusta, have the bride look through the photo album of my past cakes—it should be on top of my desk."

"Got it," her aunt said.

"And try to get some idea what she wants. General idea of color, theme, flowers if you can. And get a rough guest count."

"Okay."

"Since the wedding's not until the end of November, I can meet with her later this fall to hammer out details. That gives her time to choose bridesmaid dresses and nail down exact colors, and I'll have lots more time when Starlight Point closes for the season."

"How's it going over there? You tear out your hair yet?"

Gus grinned to herself. Her aunt already knew the answer to that question. "It's only opening day, so I still have all my hair. But

I must've lost my mind to think I could do this."

"Busy?"

"Insanity."

They said goodbye and disconnected. Gus opened her eyes. When she saw the man sitting on the other side of her picnic table, she sucked in a deep, steadying breath.

"Insanity?" Jack Hamilton asked.

"It's not polite to listen to private conversations," Gus said.

"But I was sitting right here. Hard to miss."

Gus sat up, took off her hat and pulled out the rubber band holding her ponytail. She ran her fingers through her hair, massaging the stress out of her scalp.

"Running three bakeries is tough," Gus admitted.

"I know what you mean," Jack muttered. He swung his long legs up on the seat beside him. "My feet are killing me. Wrecked my favorite shoes last night, and these are the backups."

He loosened his tie and played with it. Gus flashed to last night's embrace. She'd been thinking about his arms around her and his comment about saving Starlight Point. Did it need to be saved? She took a stab in the dark.

"Sounds like we have some of the same problems."

Jack met her eyes. "What keeps you up at night?"

"Debt," she said, more honestly than she'd intended. "Terrifying, head-over-heels, five-minutes-from-bankruptcy debt. All balancing on the hope that it'll pay off. Somehow."

Jack dropped his eyes and flushed deep red. He undid the top button on his white dress shirt.

It was hot. Even in the shady break area. There was no one around, everyone too busy to stop working. Gus untied her apron and pulled it over her head. Cool relief hit her throat and chest.

"Are you—I mean, is Aunt Augusta's Bakery—deep in debt?" Jack asked.

Gus smiled at him, enjoying the fact that she was making him nervous. She wasn't usually given to wicked delight in dangling people over the flames, but Jack had a way of activating her fight-or-flight instinct.

He took off his jacket and laid it on the table on top of her apron.

"Are you—I mean, is Starlight Point—deep in debt?" she asked.

Jack unbuttoned his cuffs and rolled up his sleeves.

"You haven't answered my question," he said.

"You'll have to ask me a different one."

Jack glanced around the break area. "Okay. How about my mother's plans for the STRIPE this year?"

Gus grinned. This was too much fun. If she made him any more uncomfortable, he'd be down to his underwear in ten minutes.

"Kissing lessons," she said matter-of-factly. "Your mother thinks all employees should be excellent and proficient—" she met his eyes "—kissers."

Jack kicked off his loafers, exposing his neat navy blue socks. "Very funny."

"I thought so," Gus said.

He exhaled loudly through his nose, sounding like a frustrated animal. His relaxed posture and half-undone clothing contrasted with tired eyes and a tight jaw. It was hard to tell when Jack was relaxed and when he was about to take off like a roller coaster.

"Did you get any sleep last night?" he asked.

Gus knew she must have slept at least some, although she didn't feel like it. The memory of a vivid dream in which she and Jack rode endlessly on the Silver Streak, laughing uproariously as the wind whipped her hair... Well, she must have been asleep a little while to have dreamed that.

Before she could put together an answer, Jack's cell phone rang. He reached for his waist clip. It wasn't there. He dug in his pants pockets. The ringing continued. Gus reached in the pocket of his jacket and handed him the phone.

"Thanks," he said quickly, looking at the caller ID and opening the phone.

"Jack Hamilton."

He listened to a loud and excited voice for a moment and said, "I'll be right there."

"Crisis in Kiddieland?" Gus asked.

"Chaos at the Sea Devil. I swear we put in miles of queue lines, but it's not enough. People are lined up on the midway, causing a major traffic jam and at least one fight."

Jack searched under the bench for his shoes and slid into them. He stood, pulling on his suit jacket and tucking the phone back in his pocket. He towered over Augusta, tense but not moving. She held her breath for a second. Two seconds.

He sighed and turned to leave.

"Jack. Wait."

He stopped in his tracks and turned. Gus got up and stood within inches of him. She buttoned his top button and snugged up his tie. Patting his shoulder, she said, "Good luck with the sea monster."

"Devil," he muttered as he walked away.

CHAPTER TEN

EARLY IN THE MORNING, almost two full weeks after opening day, silence dominated the empty queue lines. No carousel music played, no vendors rolled up their awnings, no park employees shuffled past. Gus, alone in the Midway Bakery, heard quiet footsteps at the back door. Jack Hamilton. She'd been waiting for him, knowing it was only a matter of time until their paths crossed and knowing, too, that he had the upper hand. He owned the place and he knew where to find her if he wanted to see her.

They hadn't spoken since opening day. She and Jack had exchanged only a few glances, each of them too busy or too unsure what to say. Or both.

One evening the previous week, she watched from her loft window downtown as a lone kayaker splashed soundlessly across the bay. She guessed it was him even before he reached the dock and climbed out of the boat, stretching and staring across the water at Starlight Point. He stood below her on the docks for almost ten minutes then looked up at her window, but the sunset turned the whole building orange and pink on that side. She knew from experience he would only see the reflecting sunset, not her standing alone at her window.

Now he stood just inside her bakery. He wore his summer uniform—suit, white shirt, tie, name tag simply saying *Jack*. But his expression was that of a man who didn't want to tell someone he'd accidentally backed into their car. Or needed to borrow their car.

"I have to ask a favor," he said. No good-morning, no small talk. Gus shrugged it off. He was busy, with a company to run. And so was she.

"Happy birthday, Jack."

"Thanks." He took off his jacket and hung it on a wall hook. "I'd ask how you knew, but I think everybody knows everything around here."

Gus adjusted the digital controls on the doughnut fryer. Jack took an apron from the hook next to his jacket and pulled it on. She watched him, wondering when he was going to pick up a pastry bag and ask for a job.

"Your mother told me," she said, keeping her voice neutral. "About your birthday." She wanted to ask him what the heck he was doing, but waited for him to explain. He looked as if he might grab his coat and run out the door at any minute. "Your sister asked for the morning off to pick up your other sister at the airport."

"Of course. I'm sure my mother will ride along, too."

"But not you?"

"I would be the luggage boy and couldn't get a word in all the way home. I'll see them later."

"Do you plan to wear that?" Gus asked. She pointed at her company apron, which was so short, it made him look like a giant.

Jack moved closer. "For a little while, I thought you might have been serious about the STRIPE plan."

"I am. I'm the sergeant this year."

"But it's not a kissing lesson."

"Got me. It's birthday cakes."

"I know. I came in early today to see if I can get a private lesson."

Gus wouldn't mind giving Jack a few lessons. Perhaps one in contract negotiation. Or maybe she'd stick with kissing. It seemed to have more possibilities.

"Today is my mother's birthday, too. I thought it would be nice to make her a cake."

His expression was pure vulnerability. He was so handsome in the white shirt and apron. And he needed her help. She was tempted to charge him ten grand and ten percent more than she'd charge anyone else for a cake, but she couldn't give him a hard time. It was his birthday and he wanted to bake a cake for his mother, despite everything else he probably had to do. *Darn. That's cute.*

Gus crossed the back room and stood behind Jack. She grabbed the strings of his apron and pulled them tight, tying them securely. She didn't want to look him in the eye right now, afraid she would reveal too much. Like the fact that she'd had to work very hard *not* to think about him lately.

"I'm the only one here this morning, so no one can testify that you actually made the cake yourself."

"I think my mother will be happy anyway when I show up to dinner tonight with a cake for her. Dad always ordered a special one from a bakery."

Gus pulled open the door of a large freezer and looked inside.

"It's her first birthday without Dad." Jack's voice almost wavered.

"Yours, too."

He cleared his throat and fiddled with the switch on the power mixer. "So I want it to be special for her."

"I'm going to take it easy on you," Gus said, keeping her back to him so she wouldn't get all soft just seeing his face, "since it's your birthday and all. I'm going to let you use one of my frozen cakes, so all you have to do is frost and decorate it."

"I have the feeling you're making a pretty generous offer," Jack said.

"Going to save you at least an hour—by the time you mix it, bake it and let it cool, the park will be open and you might have to run off to resolve some serious crisis. I don't want you tied to the kitchen when the curtain falls down at the Midway Theater or things get ugly at the bumper cars."

"Thanks."

"Chocolate or white?"

"Chocolate or white?" Jack looked down, tugging at his apron straps. He took off his watch and put it in his pocket. "Which one do you think my mother would like better?"

"You don't know?"

"Hey, I remembered her birthday. I can't remember everything."

"Very funny. I think you should go with chocolate."

"Why?"

Gus couldn't tell him that his mother had already baked a white cake for him. Virginia had met her at her downtown bakery last evening and together they'd decorated a respectable birthday cake.

She shrugged. "Women prefer chocolate."

"Is that a scientific study you've conducted at your bakery?"

"Nope. I made it up. Now, do you want my help or not?"

"Desperately."

"Wash your hands."

Gus felt Jack's eyes on her as she laid out pastry bags, silver tips, plastic couplers to hold the tips and spatulas. She set out several clean, damp washcloths. If he wanted to stare at her, she wondered, why had he made no attempt to come near her since opening day? Not that she'd been particularly nice to him that afternoon. Maybe it was the heat. Maybe it was the heat he stirred in her nerves whenever he was close enough to touch.

And he was close enough now. In the back room of the Midway Bakery, there was just enough space for two people to work without bumping into each other. If they were careful. She couldn't decide if she wanted to be careful or not.

"Not sure where to start," Jack said as Gus plunked two partially thawed chocolate cakes in front of him. "I'm at your mercy."

"I know. I'm enjoying that while I decide whether to make you mix your own icing."

"Could I use the power tools?"

"Industrial mixer."

"Sounds great. I always like using Mel's tools when we're out working on the rides."

"You work on rides?"

"Usually only in the off-season because I'm too busy during the summer. I like getting my hands dirty."

"No dirt here, but you might get very sticky."

"Doesn't sound so bad," he said.

Jack stood very close. She forced herself to

remember this was business. She was a vendor. He was the owner. Who hadn't crossed her threshold in two weeks. And he was only here today because he needed her. And he knew she believed in the power of birthday cakes. He was taking advantage of her.

She had baking and icing to do in the hours before Starlight Point opened. Did he think she got here this early for fun? Perhaps it hadn't occurred to him that the early morning was the busiest time for a bakery. He was being selfish, nearsighted, clueless. And standing very close.

She turned and pulled a plastic container of premade icing off the shelf.

"You might like using tools, but I don't have all day. I've got doughnuts and fresh pastries to make before the crowds roll in. I'm letting you slide on some of the details—not because you deserve it, but because I'm busy. And it's your mother's birthday. And your birthday."

"Thank you. I owe you."

Gus pulled the lid off and handed him a large pastry bag and a steel spatula. "Turn down the top of that bag to make a cuff, fill it halfway, twist it closed. I'll get some colored icing in a bag for the decorations. What color?"

"Color?"

"Your mother's favorite color. What is it?"

Jack frowned, awkwardly cuffing the pastry bag and trying to get icing to stay on the spatula long enough to make it into the bag. "Tough one. My mother likes lots of colors."

"In that case, I'd go with purple. Always a classic. I'm a big fan of pink—"

"I know. I've seen your van." He grinned at her, the smile deepening into a dimple on one side. That dimple was irresistible. *Business*, she thought, *keep this relationship business only or it'll be messier than a pie fight.*

"But pink doesn't show up very well on a cake."

"You're the boss."

Gus rolled her eyes. "Watch me. I'll do this sample cake. Step by step."

She squeezed a row of icing around the sides of the cake, spinning it expertly on a turntable. Then she iced the top, using the edge of an offset spatula to smooth the icing. She spun and scraped until an even coat of perfect white covered the cake like an overnight snowfall. It took her less than two minutes. Jack watched with great attention the whole time.

"Your turn," she said, sliding her cake off the turntable and shoving it toward him.

He lifted his cake, setting it on the turntable as if it were wired for detonation. Then he picked up the bag of icing and started to squeeze. Icing oozed out the top of the bag and over his hands, plopping onto the counter.

"You forgot to twist it closed and hold it. You do that with one hand and turn the cake with the other," she said, smiling. "Piece of cake. Easy as pie. Like stealing candy from a baby."

Jack groaned.

"I've got plenty of metaphors involving sweets. Goes with the job," Gus explained. "Also, I went to culinary school."

Jack scooped up icing and put it back in the bag.

"Did you go to how-to-run-an-amusement-park school?" she asked.

"I wish I had."

His hands were a sticky mess and icing covered his apron and the counter. Gus took a deep breath and glanced at the clock. Time was getting short.

"Wash your hands and try again," she said. "I'll help."

She guided him, laying her fingers gently over his, warm skin under the pads of her fingertips. She stood within the circle of his arms, directing the pastry bag and spinning the turntable. His scent—soap and aftershave—enclosed her.

"That's good," she said quickly, slipping out from the half circle of his arms. "Now just smooth it out."

"Easier said than done," he muttered. The distance between them was so small she could see the details of his brown eyes, his lashes, one little silver hair mixed with the dark brown at his temple.

"You can handle this," she whispered. She hoped Jack didn't realize she was speaking to herself as much as to him.

He leaned closer. Gus heard music. *Music?* Someone had started the carousel on the midway. She jerked back.

"One hour until opening," Jack said. "We always start it early. Nothing to worry about."

"Nothing to worry about?" She shoved him back two feet. "You've obviously never worked in a bakery. I'm out of time and you have to go."

Jack looked floored.

"Gus, I think you know how I…how much I…"

She held up both hands, afraid she didn't have the strength for what he was about to say. "No time, Jack."

His mouth twisted to the side, a look of concentration on his face. "Wait. I have to finish my cake."

"You'll have to prove your cake skills some other time."

Anger flashed in his eyes. "It's not about proving myself," he said. "I really wanted to…" He huffed out an angry breath and tried to untie the apron's knot behind his back. Jack fought the unseen tie, his shoulders working and head twisted unnaturally.

Gus let him struggle as a good thirty seconds counted off on the clock behind his head. A bead of sweat rolled down his forehead and nose, killing her composure. She couldn't help herself. She giggled then lost control, bursting into laughter.

"Stop it. Not funny. And if you make me

laugh, I sure won't be able to get out of this stupid apron."

"It looks nice on you."

He stopped struggling and spread his arms, grinning and flexing his muscles. "You like it?"

Gus willed herself to be cool. "Turn around," she said. "I want you out of my apron and out of my shop."

"Technically it's my shop."

"But I've paid good money to lease it," she said. "*Twenty* thousand and *twenty* percent." She was tempted to write that on his mother's cake. Not that she would. Birthday cake was a powerful tool, not to be unleashed unless you really meant business. Besides, she wondered if his mother knew anything about the contract changes. She suspected Evie knew but was staying out of it.

"What about my mother's birthday cake?"

"I'll make one this afternoon when it slows down here," she said, loosening the knot behind him. "You can pick it up later. You can even lie and say you made it."

"I don't lie," he said, turning to face her now that the apron hung loose.

Gus scrunched her lips. "You don't? Good

to know. In that case, I have a question for you. Why did you void your father's verbal contracts with all the vendors and jack up our rates for the summer?"

Jack's lips thinned into a straight line, all humor gone from his face and eyes. Gus wondered if she'd gone too far with that one.

He pulled the apron over his head, stalked over to the wall and hung it up where he'd found it. He rolled down his sleeves and buttoned his cuffs with deliberate movements. He pulled his suit jacket on, his back to her. Then his foot was out the door, his shoulders square.

Crap. This was no way to start the day. Today of all days.

"Jack," she said.

He paused and half turned in her direction. She doubted he could see her clearly now that he was in the sunny break area out back.

"Happy birthday."

CHAPTER ELEVEN

THE EARLY AFTERNOON was quiet. Gus wiped the counter, took inventory, planned for the big Saturday crowd and enjoyed a moment of peace to watch the passersby on the sunny midway.

She stood, elbows on the counter, lost in thought, when a woman whose eyes were familiar somehow faced her. The woman's glance dropped to Gus's name tag.

"I thought that must be you," she said, "even before I read your name tag."

Gus took an instant liking to the tall, graceful woman. "I'll go first. Based on your looks, I think you must be June Hamilton. Also, I heard you were here for the weekend."

June stuck out her hand. "I'm sure you must be Augusta Murphy based on the fact that you are the beautiful woman who runs the Midway Bakery."

Gus took her hand. "Has your sister, Evie, been talking about me?"

"A little, but it was Jack who provided details. He sent me to fetch Mom's birthday cake. I'm glad to dodge the bullet and not have to make one myself."

"Your sister has gotten really good at baking. You could learn, too, if you get a summer job here. Your mom's idea."

"The STRIPE," June said, rolling her eyes.

"I'll grab the cake," Gus said. "I finished it a while ago and boxed it up."

By the time Gus plucked the cake from the fridge and got back to the front, Evie had joined her sister.

"Weird to be on this side of the counter," Evie said.

The sisters didn't look exactly alike, but their relationship to each other, and Jack, was obvious. June's hair was a much lighter shade of brown than Jack's, but her eyes were copies of his. In coloring, June was a steppingstone from her older brother to her younger sister, Evie, whose blond hair and green eyes set her apart.

Lucky Jack, to have two sisters he seemed close to. And his parents nearby all his life until the recent loss of his father. Maybe he thought he had it rough because he had a big amusement park to run and family to answer to, but Gus would take those problems any day. She'd never known the sense of belonging she was starting to feel at Starlight Point.

"I'm trying to drag Evie on the new ride," June said. "But no luck."

Evie picked up the cake. "I think we should be talking business."

"Are you two planning to steal your brother's power?" Gus asked.

"Ha," June said. "Who'd want it? Too much stress."

"We're having the final meeting with the estate lawyer while June's home," Evie said. "Signing papers and transferring ownership—officially—from our parents to the three of us."

"Lucky us," June grumbled.

Evie frowned at her sister and then turned a half smile on Gus. "Thanks for making Mom's birthday cake. Jack told us what happened when he came in earlier."

Heat colored Augusta's cheeks. "He did?"

"Said you ran out of time. I told him he was a ninny for thinking you'd be free in the morning. He's obviously never been behind the counter of a bakery," Evie said.

"Men," June added.

ALTHOUGH GUS WORKED six days a week at Starlight Point, she spent Mondays at her downtown bakery in Bayside. It was the slowest day at the Point, but a surprisingly busy day in the city.

For the past three weeks, she'd juggled her time, materials and employees like a circus clown. Every night, she climbed into bed so exhausted she wondered how she'd make it all summer with this routine.

It was almost seven o'clock now, the evening fading and streaks of warm colors over the bay beginning to suggest the sunset. Gus was out for dinner with some of the vendors—their weekly meals were becoming a summer tradition—and Aunt Augusta had joined the group tonight.

"I love these paninis," Aunt Augusta said. "We used to call them grilled cheese, but *panini* sounds like something really special."

"It's the bread," Gus said. "Wish I'd thought of serving sandwiches and chips by the water.

The Dockside Grille is doing a heck of a business. Even on a Monday night."

Tosha scrunched her lips and glanced at Gus before taking a bite and chewing slowly. "Just how many irons in the fire you think you can handle?"

"One or two less than I already have."

"I was afraid of that, but it's wonderful to have you as a vendor this year," Tosha said. "Your pastries are delicious, and you're much better company than the baker who retired last year."

"Thanks," Gus said. Her cheeks warmed and she smiled.

"Maybe I could add some different sandwiches to my menu—like these paninis," Hank said. "But I'm doing all right as it is."

Tosha chatted with Augusta's aunt while the three men talked about previous summers at the Point and how this one compared. Gus listened, the chatter driving away her loneliness. Most nights she ate alone, microwaving a bowl of soup she was usually too tired to eat anyway. Her aunt had invited her to live in her small ranch house on a back street in Bayside, but Gus wanted to establish herself permanently. And that meant committing to her own place, lonely or not.

Spending time with the vendors showed Gus what it was like to belong somewhere, to share a past and possibly a future with people who weren't going anywhere. Just last week the vendors hosted a group meeting with a supplier who could save them all money if they put their orders together for next year. She hoped there would be a next year, for all of them.

Hank was in the middle of a story about a hot-dog-eating contest staged at Starlight Point years before. Judging from their expressions, she could guess the other vendors had heard this story a dozen times. But they were friends; they listened anyway.

"We could catch the seven-thirty ferry back," Bernie suggested when the story ended. Nearly everyone had finished their food except Gus and her aunt. They'd arrived late after closing her bakery just up the hill. "I want to check the day's receipts and see how my summer hire is handling the shop while I'm out partying."

"I could head back," Hank agreed.

Tosha squeezed Gus's shoulder. "See you tomorrow," she said.

The vendors walked over to the ferry dock and lined up for the ten-minute ride to the marina at Starlight Point. Like Augusta, they kept a close eye on their cash drawers and their livelihood. But Gus was lucky to have Evie—she could trust her with the job of tallying up the day's receipts.

"Got some nice friends," Aunt Augusta commented. She reached across the table and laid her hand on Gus's. "Maybe I ought to fuss over you, tell you to get a lot more sleep and start having a lot more fun. Starlight Point has a certain reputation."

"For what?"

"You know. Romance. Can't tell you how many couples here in Bayside met at the Point."

"I think the vendors are all taken," Gus said.

"I don't mean them."

Gus sighed, dipping a kettle chip in ketchup and looking over the water. "I'll keep my eyes open."

A yellow kayak caught her attention, slicing rapidly across the bay as though the rower was trying to outrun a sea monster. Arms flashed, wielding a paddle in a rhythmic motion that suggested years of practice. Although he was halfway across the bay, Gus knew it was Jack. She'd seen his kayak several times now—and not many people kayaked the bay anyway. Sailboats and powerboats were far more common.

"Looks like he's heading our way," Aunt Augusta said.

"Who?"

"You know who I mean. I see him out there rowing a lot. Virginia says he has too much stress and that's his way of working it off. I think there are more fun ways to blow off nerves."

"Seems to me like he's got the ideal job."

Aunt Augusta raised her eyebrows and cocked her head to one side. "Think so? You're losing sleep running three bakeries. Imagine what it'd be like to run the whole show."

Gus watched Jack's kayak slide along the dock. He pulled a small rope from under his feet and looped it around a cleat.

"You heard any rumblings about Starlight Point selling out to the big outfit, Consolidated Amusement Parks?"

Gus's attention snapped from Jack's kayak to her aunt. "No. But it feels like something's up. The other vendors and I have been trying to put the pieces together. Why are you asking about Consolidated?"

"They were in the shop this week, wearing their company polo shirts. Made a lot of noise about the Starlight Point cookies. Asked a lot of questions."

"I wonder," Gus said.

A buyout from a corporation that already owned at least ten amusement parks nationwide could mean she was looking at her one and only season as a vendor at Starlight Point. And this might be Jack's one and only season as the man in charge.

"Jack!" Aunt Augusta called as he hoisted himself onto the dock. "Come and join us."

He held his hand over his eyes and looked their direction.

"What are you doing?" Gus whispered. She glanced at the ferry dock. Her friends were in line, waiting to get on the ferry that was just tying up. They would have a clear view of Jack if he came to the table.

"Inviting some entertainment over. Nothing strange about it," she whispered as Jack headed their way, his long legs quickly closing the distance. "He's the son of one of my best friends. I'm practically his aunt."

"You're *my* aunt," Gus said. "You're supposed to be on my side."

"Maybe I am."

Gus shot her aunt a look, then nodded at Jack. He wore a short wet suit, but plenty of long leg showed beneath it.

She turned and watched her friends get on the boat. Even in the fading light, she saw Bernie nudge Tosha and point toward the table where Jack stood over Gus and her aunt.

"Would you mind if I grabbed some food and joined you? I don't think I've eaten since Friday. At least not that I remember."

"Of course not. Go ahead," Gus said quickly. She hoped her friends would see Jack *leave* the table and assume she'd told him to go away. She hated feeling as though she had to choose sides.

He walked toward the wide awning with *Dockside Grille* painted on it. Aunt Augusta patted her niece's hand. "See how easy that was?"

"What?"

"Getting a dinner date with a sexy man."

"It's not a date."

"It will be as soon as I make an excuse and leave you two alone."

"Don't you dare. You invited him, you can help entertain him."

"Where's the fun in that?"

"Jack and I don't exactly have a fun relationship."

"Why not? Don't tell me you've still got your panties in a twist over the contract. You're making money anyway."

"That doesn't justify going back on his father's deal," Gus said. "And I have to consider the other lease vendors. They've made me a part of their family, and they asked me to speak for them. Not that I did a very good job of that. They probably think I'm a traitor."

"Maybe his father's deal was more complicated than you know. Probably got a lot more debt than you do. Maybe that's why Consolidated is nosing around," Aunt Augusta said.

Jack strode toward them with a bottle of soda in his hand. Gus rearranged her kettle chips on the red-and-white parchment square in her basket.

Instead of sitting across the table with her aunt, he sat right next to Gus. The metal feet of his chair squawked on the concrete as he sat down and scooched the chair closer to her.

"Going to steal some of your chips while I wait for mine," he said. "I'm starving."

"Be my guest."

He leaned even closer and reached in front of her, taking a chip and dipping it in her small pool of ketchup.

"The kitchen's backed up. Guess they didn't expect such a crowd on a Monday night. Said it might be twenty minutes or so."

Jack alternated between Gus's chips and his drink for a minute. Gus alternated between giving her aunt loaded looks and watching Jack as he ate. The ferry was barely within sight now, so she could finally relax.

"Ms. Murphy," he said, "I'm wondering something."

"You should call me Aunt Augusta. Everyone does."

"Okay. Aunt Augusta, I have a question about my mother."

"Shoot."

Jack fiddled with the label on his soda bottle. "You've known her a long time. Do you think she's…uh…doing okay?"

Great. On top of his charm and smile, he cares about his mother. Gus wondered if that would soften the other vendors' attitude toward him. Maybe, but not ten thousand bucks' worth.

Aunt Augusta ran her tongue over her teeth, looking at the bay for a while. "Wish I could say I've known her well for a long time. We served on some committees together over the years, but it's really been in the last year we've gotten to be friends."

"She's mentioned your work on the Red Cross and Big Sisters program."

"We stay busy. As for how she's handling the change in her life, it's hard to say. She's lucky to have you and your sisters. When the summer's over and things simmer down at the Point, I think she's gonna need a friend. I'll make sure she stays busy with our committee work next fall and winter. Nothing like helping other people to make you feel better yourself."

"Thanks. My sister June asked me how she was doing, and I wasn't sure what to say. Evie probably knows her best anyway."

"Order 243," the lady at the counter yelled.

"Is that you?" Gus asked.

"Wishful thinking. I'm 256."

"Good thing I have plenty of chips left."

"You're nicer than my sisters," Jack said. "They never surrender their food willingly." He took a sip of his drink. "How about you? Any brothers or sisters?"

"Nope. Just me."

"And you didn't go to school in Bayside—but your parents lived here?"

"We all lived here, but I went to Catholic school up to eighth grade. Then my father transferred to a different plant. I went to high school near Detroit."

"And they're in China for five years now," Jack said.

Gus looked up, surprised. "How did you know?"

"Evie told me."

"Oh. They lived here again while I went to culinary school and then worked for a while in Boston."

"Lucky me," Aunt Augusta said, "she was ready to come home and open her own place."

Gus smiled at her aunt. "I'm the lucky one. Aunt Augusta kept me from being a lonely kid. I must have made a hundred birthday cakes with her before I was twelve years old."

"That's a lot of birthdays," Jack said.

"All of my dolls and stuffed animals had a birthday at least three times a year. I had a calendar to keep them all straight." Gus hadn't shared that story in a long time. Jack listened as if she were the most important person on earth.

"Very creative."

"Not really. Animals age faster than humans. In teddy-bear years, I'm old enough to retire," Gus said.

Aunt Augusta laughed. "I would've been put out to pasture ages ago in that case."

"Order 256," the counter lady yelled.

"Hallelujah," Jack said. "I was about to embarrass myself by stealing food from neighboring tables."

JACK ASSESSED THE evening sky as he picked up his dinner from the order window. If he didn't get back in his kayak in the next ten minutes, he wouldn't make it to the dock at his house on the Old Road before dark. No lights on his kayak meant no nighttime navigation.

The food in the basket—a grilled ham-and-cheese panini—smelled delicious. Even more tempting was the lady at the table, the evening glow washing her face and hair with warm light.

He'd never been a man who insisted on having his cake and eating it, too. Lately, he hadn't even managed to have any cake because his life was being eaten up by Starlight Point. Not that he minded, but…

Jack had a tough choice. Take his food to go or enjoy the company of Gus and her aunt. Maybe he had no choice. After all, he did owe Gus a half order of his chips. As for getting home? He'd figure it out.

"What'd you get?" Aunt Augusta asked, checking out his basket. "Is that the grilled ham-and-cheese sandwich?"

"Panini," Gus said.

The sun dipped even lower, going behind a cloud and sending a deep shadow over the dock.

"Looks like you're going to need a ride home," Aunt Augusta said.

"Can I hope you'll take me?"

She laughed. "I'm worried about my spotless reputation. And my car's way too small for your kayak. Now, Gus here doesn't have any reputation to speak of and she has a big van. Her parents are out of town, but I'll give her permission to go home with a nice young man like you."

"Thanks a lot," Gus said. She shoved back from the table, not quite making eye contact with Jack. "I'll pull my van down here and we'll put your kayak in the back."

"I don't want to be a pain in the neck if you...had other plans."

Gus finally met his eyes. "It's my night off. I usually rescue stranded boaters and feed the hungry on Mondays. Be right back."

"I'll hit the road, too," Aunt Augusta said. "Boss expects me in first thing tomorrow. G'night, kids."

Jack watched Gus and her aunt climb the slight grade to the street and turn the corner. A small parking lot was down one block, taking the place of an old building that had met the wrecking ball years ago. He finished his sandwich and drink and headed for his kayak, untying it and pulling it up on the dock to drip dry.

When he'd gotten into his kayak two hours

earlier, he would never have imagined his evening ending like this. A few months ago, he would never have imagined that he'd meet someone like Augusta.

CHAPTER TWELVE

MOST DINERS WERE gone and quiet settled over the docks as Gus backed her van down the narrow driveway. Keeping her eye on the side mirrors, she aimed for the dock with a yellow kayak.

Putting the van in Park, Gus didn't even unbuckle her seat belt before Jack opened the rear doors. He balanced the one-man kayak on his shoulder as if he'd done it a thousand times.

"Tried to dry it off some," he said. He loaded it and shut the door. "Do I get to drive?"

"Sorry." Gus laughed. "You're not on my insurance plan."

Jack gripped the collar of his wet suit and peeled it down his body. Gus leaned against the cool back door of her van and tried to concentrate on the last rays of the sunset without focusing on the broad chest being revealed inch by inch in front of her. She looked away—okay, she *intended* to look away—as he shucked the wet suit over his hips and down his legs, revealing a pair of dark blue swim trunks underneath.

"Do I seem dangerous?" he asked.

"Very," Gus breathed. "You get to navigate. And no honking the horn this time."

"No problem."

"Do you have a shirt?" she asked after he climbed in the passenger seat next to her. "The seat belt's going to chafe, but you have to wear it. Company policy."

"I'll tough it out," he said, tugging it on.

Gus dug into a box behind her seat and pulled out a pink T-shirt. "Here," she said. "We had these made for our employees, but no one needed the extra large." She handed him the shirt, which had the company logo screen-printed on the front: *Aunt Augusta's Bakery* over an elaborate three-tiered cake.

"I match your van," Jack said as he put on the shirt and leaned out to admire himself in the side mirror.

"And if you ever need a job, you've already got the uniform."

"You've seen my cake-decorating skills," he said.

"I believe in second chances." The words slipped out before she could think. She wished she could gauge his reaction, but she was afraid to look at him. Instead, she came to a full stop at the top of the hill, driving as if she were taking the test to get her license.

The drive took only ten minutes—no cars were heading toward the amusement park at this time of night. To break the silence as they crossed the Point Bridge, Gus was tempted to ask if Jack was selling Starlight Point, but close quarters weren't the best place for dropping bombshells.

"I'm sorry—you're going to get in a lot of traffic when you turn around to head home," Jack said.

"I'm getting used to it. But I've never driven down your street," she said. "I didn't realize how close the Old Road homes are to the Point."

"Right next door. I risk my life every day walking across the parking lot to get to work. Maybe I should have pedestrian lanes painted and crosswalks installed."

"Lately," Gus said, "I've been taking some risks, too. Bought a van, took out a loan the size of Lake Huron, opened a bakery, and you know the rest."

Jack was silent a few minutes. Huge homes came and went in the van's headlights.

"There's my house. The small one. Driveway's just past the mailbox."

"No mansion?"

"Disappointed?"

"I'm hardly in a position to judge. I'm living in a flat above my bakery."

She cut the engine. He took off his seat belt.

"I'm no genius in the kitchen, but I could offer you a piece of leftover birthday cake if you'll come in for a while."

Gus hesitated. This was a decisive moment. Back out of the driveway or take a chance? The flutter in her chest could be telling her either one.

"I know it's a few days old, but I kept it in the fridge," he said.

Gus toyed with the keys dangling from the ignition, but her glance strayed to Jack's long fingers resting on his bare thighs.

"I also make excellent coffee. I learned the summer I worked the coffee shop at the hotel."

"Coffee shop?"

He nodded. "Yep. Parents insisted. We all had to work seasonal jobs so we'd see things from a different perspective."

"I knew Evie did that, but I somehow didn't picture you slugging it out every day with the minimum-wage crowd."

"Because I'm the oldest son? That's a pretty medieval assumption."

"Maybe."

"Believe me, if you'd known me the year I shoveled coal on the train crew, you'd never have imagined I was the boss's son."

"Dirty?"

"Filthy. But I had dangerous muscles."

Gus tried not to think about Jack covered in sweat, muscles—dangerous or not—rippling under bare flesh.

"Only did that one summer. My parents were afraid I'd run off with a train girl."

"So no big summer romances for you?"

"Nothing serious." He leaned close and whispered, "I've always been in love with Starlight Point."

Okay, so maybe he wasn't going to sell out. You couldn't sell something you loved. Unless you had to.

"I think I'd like some cake and coffee," Gus said.

Jack's home was a total surprise. One story, large uncurtained windows in the living room overlooking Starlight Point. Nothing on the walls. Small television hung directly across from the only furniture—a lumpy brown couch. Kitchen and serving bar to one side.

"Not much to look at, huh?" he asked. "Had this place five years and haven't changed much. Seems to work."

"It's uncomplicated. Simple."

"Glad you see it that way. No sense in a fancy place when I practically live at the Point. My mother can't imagine how I sleep in this 'hovel,' as she calls it. My sisters think I should at least hang some pictures. But I think..." He gestured out the back windows where the twilight sky was punctuated by the coaster lights.

"With a view like that, who needs artwork?" Gus suggested.

"You understand," he said, stepping behind her and laying one hand on her shoulder. He put his other hand gently at her waist, barely touching her. She watched a lighted train climb slowly up a hill and then crest and fall, racing away into the night. A line of cars waited to exit the lot, their drivers impatient after a long day in the park. Lights stretched across the Point Bridge, a ribbon of red and white indicating the nightly traffic jam.

Jack cleared his throat. His lips brushed her temple. He smelled of lake water and a touch of salt. It would be so easy to lean back against him and feel his arms close around her. They were alone in his living room, watching the night skyline of a place they both loved. She took a deep breath and stepped forward instead of back, reminding herself that she worked there, under his thumb and contract. What would the other lease vendors think if they could see her now? They would expect her to zap him with a rubber band and put him in his place.

She turned to tell him good-night, face-to-face, but he spoke first. "Gus, I think you know I'd like to spend more time with—"

"I should go," she said. She had to stop him before he said something she would find too hard to resist.

"But I thought—"

"It's getting late. I have to be right over there—" she pointed toward the flashing lights of the midway "—very early in the morning."

Jack's jaw tensed. "I promised you cake and coffee."

Gus tried to laugh to break the tension, but it sounded insincere, even to her. "You could come by my bakery tomorrow. Have some then."

Wailing sirens in the parking lot caught his attention. He raised his head for a second, glancing toward the large window and listening. A faint crease appeared between his eyebrows.

"I would prefer to be alone with you. We could talk."

More sirens and air horns. Jack made a visible effort to ignore the noise from the parking lot. A cell phone rang, vibrating on the kitchen table where it rested with his keys and wallet.

"Maybe you better answer that," she said. "I'll just show myself out."

Jack held out one hand in a gesture that said *wait* while he grabbed the phone, glancing at the name of the caller. "It's the chief of security." He answered the phone and listened for a minute. "Uh-huh. I was afraid of that.

Got Bayside Fire coming in?" Jack stalked over and looked out his window. "Uh-huh. Yep. Only thing you can do. I'm right here at the house. I'll open the gate."

He disconnected the call and set his phone on the table.

"Gate?" Gus asked.

"The one out of the parking lot that opens onto the Old Road. We don't usually want all that traffic going down the Old Road because it's dark and narrow and just not built for it. But no choice tonight. The Point Bridge is closed by an accident and thousands of people have to have some way off the peninsula."

"You have a gate key?"

"I own the place. I have a key to everything." Jack slipped on a pair of sneakers that were under his kitchen table. He returned to Gus, moved in close and ran a gentle finger down her cheek. The movement was personal. Too personal. It reminded her why she needed to leave now.

"You have two choices," Jack said. "You can leave now because once I open the gate onto the Old Road you'll be in the mother of all traffic jams." He moved even closer. "Or you can wait here. I'll be back in a half hour or so and you'll have to stay late because of traffic. We can pick up where we left off."

Gus thought about it. Was picking up where they left off the wisest thing to do? And where exactly did they leave off anyway? She could run now, beat the traffic and settle onto her nice, safe couch to watch television. Sleeping on the events of the evening and evaluating them in the sane morning light was a whole lot smarter than committing to a late night at Jack Hamilton's. Her aunt may not agree, but her bank loan and the other lease vendors certainly would.

"You know which choice I'm hoping for," Jack said. "We could still have that cake and coffee I promised you."

Gus shook her head. "I think I've already indulged enough tonight." She headed for the door.

"Gus, wait."

She turned, feeling braver about resisting him as she neared escape.

"Thanks for the ride home," he said. "Any chance you'll have dinner with me as a way to…uh…thank you?"

Dinner with Jack. An actual date and not a chance meeting or flirtation. That was another thing she'd have to sleep on. But she already knew what her practical side would tell her. Getting involved with the owner of Starlight Point wouldn't make it any easier for her to face her friends, pay her employees and retire her massive bank loan.

"I don't know," she said. "You have a reputation for stealing food. Having dinner with you is just—" she paused, flinching inwardly at the crestfallen look on Jack's face "—too risky for me."

As she drove down the Old Road, she glanced toward the section of parking lot Jack cut across to open a little-used access gate. His bright pink shirt picked up the headlights from an approaching security vehicle, and Gus chuckled, wondering how he'd explain his wardrobe choice if anyone asked.

EVIE TOOK OFF her silver-rimmed glasses and shoved the folder back toward Jack. She shut the laptop in front of her and sighed, frowning at her brother.

"I was afraid of this," she said.

"You were ahead of me, then. I had no clue."

"I just had a feeling these last few years.

Always wondered where some of the revenue for the capital improvements was coming from. Now we know. Dad didn't share any of this with you?"

"Nope." Jack scrubbed his fingers through his hair as he stood watching Starlight Point through his living room window.

"I thought your jobs overlapped quite a lot."

"Not really. I can see why you thought so. I'm sure everyone did. Truth is, I did my thing and he did his. I was responsible for the human resources and marketing. Got out and about, fixed problems, fixed a ride now and then when Mel let me."

"But..."

"Dad kept tight control of the books."

Evie snapped her glasses into their case. "Think Mom knew about this?"

"No."

"How could he live with her and not tell her?"

"You know how he was. Always on to the next idea, the next plan, the bigger and better ride. Probably thinking the new idea would pay off every time."

Evie joined her brother at the window. "Optimistic," she whispered, "but dangerous."

Jack crinkled his forehead. “I don’t get it. Several accountants work for us in the main office. How could they not know?”

“They probably did,” Evie said. “But accountants keep their mouths shut. It’s the number one rule they teach us in school. Otherwise they wouldn’t have a job for long.”

Jack grinned. “Does this mean you’re not telling me how Aunt Augusta’s bakeries are doing?”

“Do you want to know?”

“A little.”

Evie rolled her eyes. “I’m not telling you anything. Unless, of course, you’d consider disclosing the nature of your relationship with Gus.”

“Can’t.”

Evie smirked, one side of her mouth lifting. “Or won’t? Mom saw her van in your driveway a few nights ago. You should tell me everything.”

“Can’t,” Jack said. “Because I don’t know. Did Mom also tell you she stayed precisely five minutes?”

Evie laughed. “I guess your garage-sale bachelor pad didn’t appeal to her.”

Something clunked against Jack’s front

door. He opened it and leaned out. "Newspaper. I was hoping it was the pizza guy. Almost afraid to read the paper these days."

He unrolled it on the counter and saw a huge headline. Front page. Above the fold. Starlight Point Officially Handed Off to Next Generation, New Owners Mum on Future Plans.

"How close can a reporter get to the truth?" Evie asked.

"It's not the truth that tends to hurt you. It's the speculation. The *Bayside Reflections* loves to run articles on Starlight Point. The family curse."

"But most of the time it helps us. Even bad PR is still PR," Evie pointed out.

"We need to try to shape it, though. How about inviting them for a feature piece? Something light, interesting, unique," Jack said.

The doorbell rang again and Jack greeted the pizza guy, paying him and taking the large steaming box to the counter. He set it directly on the newspaper. Evie grabbed plates and a soda and helped herself.

"How about the STRIPE?" she asked.

"The stupid STRIPE has probably tortured half the people in Bayside. Anyone who ever worked for us. It's been driving me nuts for years."

"But in a good way. People have funny memories of the program. And it could be your friend right now. Have the paper do a feature on this year's improvement plan.

Jack bit off a huge chunk of pizza and glared at his sister.

"Think about it," Evie said. "It's a great story. Gus is a local girl who came home and started her own business. She's one of our most successful lease vendors from what I've seen so far—and I'm still not giving you details about that—and she'd give a great interview. Plus—" Evie paused "—everyone loves birthday cake."

"I'm listening."

"Mom could be featured, too. She's an interesting and sympathetic character. She could talk about all the STRIPEs over the years. The paper could interview past employees and maybe dig up some real success stories."

"I still haven't used my conversational Spanish or knitting skills," Jack said.

"Give it time. The season has only just started."

They made a dent in the large pizza as they talked through financial and marketing plans. As it got closer to ten o'clock, Evie announced she was headed in to collect the cash boxes from all the bakeshops and close them up for the night.

"Doesn't she usually do that? Except for Mondays?" Jack asked.

Evie smirked. "Very observant. And yes, she does. But she said she was going home early tonight."

"Why?"

"Since it's none of my business, I didn't ask."

CHAPTER THIRTEEN

GUS HAD THOUGHT sweet treats would help, but she'd lost control of the meeting about five minutes after it started. Almost twenty lease vendors sat on chairs pulled into a messy half circle in the front room of her shop. She'd considered holding the meeting in the workroom, but flowers and delicate decorations for a Saturday wedding were spread over the worktables. If they were damaged—or eaten—she couldn't remake them. Time was a valuable commodity this summer.

Besides, she had nothing to hide. She could host a meeting of the Starlight Point lease vendors on her own private property if she wanted to. It wasn't as if they were planning a crime. They were strategizing about their contracts and bottom lines. They had no exact plans—just a vague idea that they needed to join forces.

"You've been getting cozy with Jack Hamilton," Tosha said, her tone implying a gentle warning. "From what I hear."

"Cozy?" Gus said, feeling the charged atmosphere shift. "I'm the one who shot him with a rubber band." She tried to imply a casual coolness she was afraid she couldn't pull off. She had already given Jack too much this summer: a hug, a ride home, a private cake-decorating lesson. She'd have a hard time explaining any of these things, and especially her feelings, if this group decided to push her on it.

"Things can change," Tosha said.

Gus stood behind the counter, where she doled out leftover pastries. "One thing hasn't changed," she said, speaking slowly and clearly. "We're all working hard to make a living and deserve honest treatment. Believe me, I'm just as upset today as I was the day I read that contract and realized someone had changed the rules on us."

"Not someone," Hank said, "Jack Hamilton." He looked more serious than usual, probably because he wasn't wearing his ketchup-and-mustard-stained apron.

Gus nodded, conceding that point, although the more she knew of Jack, the more she suspected he was hiding something. What was behind his decision to go back on his father's contracts and to be so guarded about it?

"So, what are we gonna do? It's June seventh already and none of us've done nothing," Bernie said. "We still gonna be sittin' on our hands on the Fourth of July?"

"That's why we're here," Tosha said. "We need to talk about what we can do. If anything."

"Read today's paper?" Hank asked. "Big article about how the estate finally got settled by the lawyers. Mrs. Hamilton handed the whole thing over to the three kids. Lock, stock and barrel."

"Lucky kids," someone grumbled.

Gus put cookies on a wide tray. She flashed back to June's comment and wondered if the three kids did feel lucky. Taking on a massive family business right before the season opened—and the unexpected death of their father—wasn't necessarily a stroke of luck. Evie talked to Gus every day, reviewing the accounts of Aunt Augusta's three locations at the Point, but she didn't reveal many personal details. Virginia talked to Aunt Augusta frequently, but Gus suspected no family financial secrets traded hands. The Hamiltons were a closemouthed group when it came to their beloved Starlight Point.

Many of the vendors had been spending their summers at the Point for years, so there were no personal attacks on the Hamiltons. But their own businesses were on the line, and their families were depending on them. Something had to give.

"One of us should make an appointment with Jack. Set up a meeting about renegotiating our contracts," Bernie said. Twelve voices jumped in to agree. But Gus said nothing, attracting the notice of Bernie.

"You don't think so, Gus? You *like* handing over that extra cash?"

"I feel the same way you do, but I can't see that we'll have any success just asking for the contract to be reopened."

She heard the grumbles. Someone pushed back a chair, which squeaked loudly on the tile floor.

"We signed contracts," Gus continued. "Binding both sides. He's not obligated to renegotiate any more than we would be."

"But we want to," Hank said.

"But he doesn't have to."

"Whose side are you on?" Bernie asked.

"Ours. But I'm being realistic." She stood in front of the crowd, having delivered the cookies but not finding an empty chair. Her face felt hot and she talked with her hands as she tried to argue reason even while questioning her own motives.

"What can we bring to the table?" she asked. "Do we counteroffer? Make some promises?"

"Make some threats," someone grumbled.

"What kind of counteroffer?" Tosha asked.

Gus toyed with her apron strings. It was a Thursday night, and she still wore the Starlight Point apron she'd put on that morning at the Midway Bakery. Long day. And looking at this crowd, it was going to be longer.

"Well, for example, we could ask him to remove the flat fee in exchange for a larger percentage of profits."

"Or vice versa," someone suggested.

"Possibly. We'd have to take a survey and figure out what would benefit our group most. Another idea is to ask for a reduction of next year's fees," Gus suggested. She tried to keep her voice level and reasonable.

"If we come back," Hank said.

More murmuring and whispering followed that statement.

"I'm curious," Gus said. "Are your sales this year comparable to previous years? This is my first summer, as you know, so I've got nothing to compare it to."

Uncomfortable glances shifted from chair to chair.

"Well?" Gus said. "I'm not asking for numbers, but a ballpark idea."

"I'll say it," Tosha said. "Mine are actually a shade better. So far."

"Than last year?"

"Than I've ever done," Tosha said.

"Wow."

"Me, too," Bernie said. A few others nodded agreement.

"I'm not going to the bank with a wheelbarrow full of money," Hank acknowledged, "but I'm sure not doing worse than usual."

"Good weather so far this year," Bernie said. "We get a rainy spell and our profits will sag like an old lady's…" Tosha shot him a look and he clammed up.

Everyone was silent a minute. Gus still stood at the front of the group. Their chairs all faced her, and she alone could look out the front window. So she was the only one who saw a man standing just outside the circle of light cast by the bulb over her door. A tall man. A very tall man. Gus froze, guilt clutching her lungs and stealing her voice.

"You okay, Gus?" Tosha asked.

She looked at Tosha then back to the place where Jack had stood. He was gone. Clammy coolness spread down her neck, fanned across her back and down her arms. She pictured Jack's perspective of the scene in her shop. A late-night meeting across the water from Starlight Point. A mob of lease vendors—many of whom he would surely recognize even from the back. Most important, her. Standing in front of the group as if she were holding court.

What would he think? She shook her head and refocused on the circle of vendors. What did it matter what he thought? They weren't saying anything about him or their contracts that wasn't true. And just what was he doing out there anyway? Spying on them? On her?

Gus leaned against the low counter by the cash register. "Do we have a plan?" she asked.

"I liked your ideas," Bernie said. "Go to

Jack with an offer that evens the deal for us and he gets to save face."

"Second that," someone said.

"Everyone agree?" Gus asked.

Heads nodded; positive-sounding grunts followed.

"So we just have to decide two things. Exactly what do we want to offer and who are we going to send?"

"Gotta look at my books to decide the first question," Hank said.

"Uh-huh."

"Me, too."

"So, we'll meet again in a week to decide? Same time, same place?" Gus asked.

"Sounds good," Tosha said.

People got up, some of them slowly, from the hard chairs. Long days on their feet at the Point were physically and emotionally exhausting. Gus understood. She was bone-tired every night, and sometimes thoughts of her bank loan crowded much-needed sleep out of her mind.

She sent her fellow vendors home with extra cookies. Five different people invited her to a bar around the corner where they were getting together and having a drink.

Even though she relished belonging to the group, she declined. It was late. She wanted to climb the three floors to her loft and slip into bed before her brain started working out scenarios and renegotiating techniques. Maybe she could trick herself into sleeping if she refused to even think until tomorrow.

JACK'S CAR, THE battered SUV that few people would suspect him of driving, sat a few blocks down from Gus's bakery. He'd told himself he just wanted to see who was at this late-night meeting. A glimpse of the room confirmed his paranoia. It was the lease vendors, and Gus captained the ship. He'd heard raised voices, even through the windows, and retreated to his car before they saw him and came after him.

Downtown Bayside was dark and quiet on Thursday night. He watched people leave her shop, most of them munching cookies and looking satisfied. Maybe it would have been worth crashing the party. The vendors walked in groups to cars, laughing, sharing rides. Last summer, he would have joined them, had a beer at the bar around the corner. They would never have viewed him as an adversary or worse.

Things were different now.

Jack closed his eyes, thinking of his father. He sunk into the seat, leaning his head on the headrest. His eyes burned under the closed lids. Just tired, he told himself. He had no time for tears. He sunk deeper into the seat. He'd rest just a few minutes before driving home and trying to sleep.

Tapping awakened him. Quiet tapping, a bird at his bedroom window. He was in his blue bedroom in his parents' house, a Spider-Man pillow under his cheek. He was dreaming of a little bird. The tapping got louder and more insistent. The bird wanted him to wake up.

"Jack," the bird said. A talking bird? Who knew his name?

"Jack, wake up." The bird in his dream was now a tall woman with cascading brown hair and a wide smile. He opened his eyes, turning toward the voice. Gus Murphy wore an old sweatshirt, her hair a wild mess. She was not smiling.

Jack pushed the button to lower the window, but the car wasn't running, so it didn't work. He was in a fog, trying to think of how to get the window down so Gus would stop knocking and let him go back to sleep.

Gus wrinkled her forehead, walked around the front of his car, jerked open the passenger door and got in.

"What are you doing?" she asked.

"Sleeping?"

"In your car. On my street. Is this some kind of a stakeout?"

"Not anymore."

"So you were watching me. You were spying on my meeting with the vendors."

Jack rubbed his eyes, trying to think of something sensible to say that wouldn't get him in worse trouble.

"What time is it?" he asked.

"Three o'clock in the morning."

Jack thought about that a minute, trying to remember the last time he'd been out this late. Or this early.

"What are *you* doing?" he asked. "Shouldn't you be in bed? I thought bakers got up really early."

"They do. But I got tired of worrying about you out here."

"You were worried about me?"

Gus gently slapped Jack's cheek. "Are you awake yet?"

"I think there's a good chance I might be dreaming."

"You're not. I saw you watching us through the window during our meeting."

"What was that all about?"

"None of your business."

Jack took a deep breath, hoping the oxygen would restore his brain function. "Considering you're all working at my business, I might be interested."

"*At* your business. Not *for* your business."

"Okay."

Gus huffed out a breath. "We had things to discuss."

"Plotting an overthrow?"

"Yes."

Jack leaned back and closed his eyes. "I surrender. You can have it all."

He waited for something to happen, afraid to open his eyes. Gus would either take him at his word and relieve him of the burden of Starlight Point, or she would slap him back to his senses. Perhaps she'd offer him cake.

"You're a lucky man, Jack Hamilton," she whispered.

He opened his eyes. "Tell me why I'm so lucky."

"I saw you spying on us and didn't rat you out to all my fellow vendors. I saw your car sitting here at midnight, one o'clock and the hours since. And I didn't call the police and tell them there was a drunk man sleeping in his car outside my loft, making me feel threatened."

"I'm not drunk."

"But it would have been great entertainment to watch you go through a field sobriety test three floors below me. I doubt you could walk a straight line right now."

"That's because my eyes are glued shut from being so tired I fell asleep in my car."

"That's what they all say."

"So tell me," Jack said, turning in his seat and leaning close. He was gratified to note that she didn't shrink back against her door. "Why else am I so very lucky?"

"Perhaps the most important reason is this—I love your mother and I love your sister, so I'm feeling merciful. And, most important, I think I'm starting to fall in love with..."

Jack leaned closer, his lips only inches from hers.

"Starlight Point," Gus concluded, her eyes on his and a slightly wicked smile turning up the corners of her lips. "It gets under your skin and in your blood."

Jack felt his pulse racing through his brain and beating inside his ears. He knew something else that was under his skin and in his blood. And she was right there. He wanted to close the small gap between them, take her lips with his. He hadn't made out in a car in a decade, not since he was a foolish teenager, but the temptation was irresistible.

He didn't have time to finish his thought. Gus slipped her hand behind his head and pulled his lips to hers for a fast-breathing, heat-generating, stars-behind-your-eyelids kiss.

No way could he walk a straight line now, even at gunpoint.

The kiss was over as suddenly as it had begun. Gus pulled back, took a deep breath and stared him down for a minute. This was it, he thought. She was only pausing to invite him up to her place…

"Good," she said. "You're awake. I won't feel bad sending you home now."

She got out, slammed the passenger door and let herself into her building.

Jack rested his head on the steering wheel for just a moment, hoping his blood would circulate back into a regular pattern. He tugged on his seat belt and switched on the engine. If he got to bed in the next half hour, he'd get a few hours' sleep before a busy Friday gearing up for a busy weekend.

The roller coaster his life had become was a messy track of exhilarating highs, devastating lows and gut-wrenching twists. Having Augusta along for the ride upped the thrill rating to a whole new level.

CHAPTER FOURTEEN

THE MID-JUNE HEAT rolled across the counter at the Midway Bakery. Liz served up cookies and pastries to guests. Gus ran cookies through the bake ovens in the back, getting ready for the weekend. Tomorrow promised to be a busy Saturday and she wanted to keep the profits rolling in. The specialty cookies depicting rides at the Point were a bigger seller than she had even hoped. She cut out and baked two huge batches of the Sea Devil–shaped cookies, debating about which of the other ones she should stock up on.

"What do you think, Liz? Do people like the carousel, the Silver Streak, the Star Spiral or the night skyline the most? In my opinion, it's a dead heat."

"Aren't you keeping track?"

Gus shook her head. "Not really. Evie could tell me how many cookies we've sold, but we haven't kept track of what the shape is. Think we should start?"

Liz shrugged. "This seems to be working okay. We're not throwing away any cookies at the end of the day, and people seem happy."

"Which is your favorite?" Gus asked.

"Probably the Sea Devil. Love the new ride."

"Haven't tried it yet. I'm not a big fan of twisty rides," Gus said.

"You don't know what you're missing. I went on it with Evie at the first employee ride night last week. It's great in the dark."

"I'll bet."

Liz wagged a finger and grinned at Gus. "Wait a minute. Exactly how many rides have you tried at Starlight Point?"

"I've ridden quite a few."

"I mean this year," Liz said.

"Oh." Gus thought about it. The only rides she'd been on this season were with Jack. And a tandem bicycle and a maintenance cart probably didn't count. "None yet, I guess. I've been busy. And there's plenty of summer left."

"You own three bakeries here, you've made hundreds of coaster-themed cookies, and you haven't pulled down a lap bar and screamed your head off yet? If that gets out, people will call you a big fake. You'll have to come to the next ride night and live it up a little. Or I'm spilling your secret."

"Maybe," Gus said. "But I think those nights are for the younger employees. Teenagers and college students."

Liz laughed. "Nope. Everyone who's not too tired goes. There's lots of young summer employees, sure, but you'd be surprised at who else is there—some of the older maintenance guys, lease vendors, hot security guards. I even saw Jack Hamilton wearing an apron and serving drinks and French fries."

"No way," Gus said. A sight like that would make it worth her while to go to ride night.

"Really," Liz said. "I think he always goes. I remember seeing him on the rides a few years ago when I worked here for the summer. That's before I had my son. Now I don't get out much unless I'm working."

Liz turned and waited on a customer, boxing up two slices of cake with napkins neatly rolled and tied on top. She completed the sale, smiling as if it was the best job she'd ever had. Liz was a real find. She showed up on time, never complained and had a way with guests.

Gus stood in the doorway between the front and back rooms, watching the customers and trying to decide which cookies would sell best on a Saturday halfway through June. She knew this summer was shaping up to be very profitable already, despite the lack of any progress on renegotiating their contracts. The vendors had met again last night in her downtown bakery, but no one could agree on whether to negotiate the flat fee or the percentage part of the contract.

They wanted Gus to be the arbiter, but her leadership was lackluster. Her heart wasn't in it. She couldn't complain about her sales, and she liked the Hamilton family. But she couldn't say that to the other vendors. The evening ended with a stalemate, no decision on approaching Jack. They planned to meet again, but Gus doubted a week would make much difference in her resolve or their organization.

She wondered if a week might strengthen her resolve to avoid getting entangled with the man who'd started the whole mess. Impulse and a generous serving of desire had made her lock lips with him in his car. But she'd come to her senses a half second before the kiss turned dangerous, making up an excuse and sending him home. Shipping him off got tougher every time he touched her, and summer rolled ahead with weeks and weeks of temptation.

She turned her attention back to the front counter, where Liz had just finished selling a whole box of treats to a group of teenagers with a maniacal roller-coaster gleam in their eyes.

"Who watches your son when you're working here?" Gus asked.

"Day care at the hotel."

"Hotel?"

"The one here," Liz said.

"The Lake Breeze Hotel?"

"Uh-huh. They just added it this summer. For employees and vendors with little kids. They didn't need that old wing of the hotel for employee dorms this year since there aren't as many employees. So, they converted part of it to a day care. I heard about it just before the park opened—that's why I applied for this job. Not many summer jobs come with free day care."

"That's amazing," Gus said. "And free?"

"Yep. There's a playroom, a lunchroom and a nap room. And I can visit Braden during my breaks. Evie said it was her brother's idea. Sure works for me no matter who came up with it."

Gus sighed. Jack had more dimensions and twists than the Silver Streak. How was she supposed to figure out a guy who put the screws to lease vendors but offered free day care to all employees—even the employees of the vendors? More important, how was she going to keep resisting him?

"We'll have to deliver some cookies sometime," Gus said. "Just for a treat."

Three maintenance guys hustled past, their tool belts swinging. One talked on his cell phone. None of them looked happy.

"Hope it's not the Sea Devil again," Liz said. "I love it, but I hear it's been broken down about as often as it's been running."

"What's the problem with it?"

"Don't know. I've heard a couple of things. One rumor said it's electronics. I also heard they didn't consider the stiff breeze that comes off the lake sometimes. Engineering flaw. I guess it stopped a train last night."

Gus laughed. "I have a hard time believing that."

"I heard it from one of the girls who loads riders on the platform. There's a steep hill that doesn't have a lift chain—just uses momentum—right by the beach. She says that strong wind we had earlier this week stopped the train and a bunch of people got stuck."

"They got the people off, though, right? Nobody got hurt or anything?" Gus asked.

"No, but it looks bad for the ride and Starlight Point in general."

"I'm sure. Nobody likes bad PR. Especially because Jack Hamilton is…" Gus paused, not sure how to put it.

"Totally trying to prove himself in the wake of his father?" Liz asked.

Gus nodded. "I'm sure he is."

"That would be tough. But he's been working here his whole life. He has to know what he's doing. He's a couple years older than me, but I had a major crush on him a few summers ago. I think every girl who works here does."

"Has he ever dated the summer employees?"

Liz laughed. "No. And it's a bummer he

doesn't. If he ever started, girls would be lined up in the ride queues. On top of being hot and rich, he has a reputation for being incredibly nice."

Jack seemed to have no trouble asking me out, Gus thought. *Maybe the rules are different for vendors. Or maybe he can do whatever he wants now that he's the owner, not just the owner's son.*

"Sounds like a perfect man," Gus said lightly.

"I've learned my lesson about the existence of that mythical creature, but Jack sure looks perfect. Even though you've had your head in the oven all season, you had to notice that."

Two more maintenance men hurried by. Liz watched them and then sent Gus a quizzical glance. "Maybe Sea Devil cookies aren't a good choice for this weekend. I'd go for the nice dependable carousel cookies if I were you." She inclined her head toward the front midway where the tinny music played. "That thing never stops."

JACK HANDED EVIE the newspaper, a scowl on his face. They sat at one of the small tables in front of the bakery in the hotel.

"Last thing we need as the season ramps up," Jack commented.

Evie had already seen the paper. A stack of them waited on the hotel counter every morning and she'd grabbed one early today. She wanted to grab them all so guests wouldn't have a chance to see the article about the problems with the new ride.

"It could've been worse," she said. "No one was injured, for one. Also, the article makes it pretty clear that it was an engineering error—the ride designer's fault—not ours."

"That doesn't really help us. Or leave us much choice. We either don't run the ride when there's a northeast wind, or we shut it down for weeks while they install an extra lift on that hill. If the work can even be done retroactively." He covered his face with his hands and rubbed his eyes with the tips of his fingers. "This is a disaster."

"Come on, Jack. It's not a disaster. It's a setback. We'll manage. Maybe something else can be done. A compromise of some kind. Have you talked to Mel Preston?"

"Last night and again this morning. He thinks we might be able to make some small adjustments to the speed and braking on some of the hills. Might do the trick, but we have to consult with the ride engineers. They're flying in tomorrow."

"See," Evie said. "It might turn out better than you think. Maybe now would be a good time for that positive PR piece. The one about the STRIPE and the birthday cakes."

"Think Gus will go along with it? I'm not at the top of the vendors' Christmas-card list. They don't like their contracts, and Gus is leading the charge."

"I can't blame them," Evie said. "No one likes surprises, especially when it involves money. You should know that better than anyone."

"I still think you should come to work in my accounting office instead of working for Gus this summer. I don't see why you're not putting family first. You know I need your help."

"One more summer, Jack. Let me have one more summer. I want to finish my master's and CPA and then I'll dive in. For now, I'm getting good experience managing the books for three pretty busy bakeries. And giving you good advice."

"Really? Let's hear it."

"Make nice with the press, ask Augusta personally to do the feature, relax for five minutes."

"What would I do without you?"

"Wait till next summer when I become your equal partner and start bossing you around. You may be wishing I'd shut up and go away."

"I wish I could fast-forward to next summer right now."

THE WEATHER FORECASTERS had hinted about evening storms, but the lake was calm. Jack told his secretary he'd have his phone with him and headed home. He crossed the parking lot with long strides, heading for his house and his kayak. Afternoons like this were made for burning off steam on the water.

He opened his mailbox and dumped its contents on the kitchen counter along with his keys, wallet and phone. The *Roller Coaster Times* leaped out at him from the junk mail. A glossy color photo of the Sea Devil took up the whole front cover with the Starlight Point insignia along the bottom. A writer from the magazine had been to the Point a month ago to test out the ride along with a few friends.

Jack flipped to the article. More pictures,

a head shot of him with a few quotes about his hopes for the season at Starlight Point. And a review of the ride. On a scale of one to four screams, it got a three and a half. The article explained that the ambience and trees along the track were good and the first two hills were totally killer, but the rest of the ride just meandered and flipped around. The reviewer thought more direct theming of the sea-monster idea would have bumped it up to four-scream level.

More sea-monster stuff? Where the heck were those writers looking? The cars were made like ships, the color of the track sea blue, and the ride platform and entrance had large signs and artwork depicting coaster riders in the clutches of a leviathan. Even the queue lines—which they'd later discovered weren't quite adequate—undulated in a wavelike pattern.

Jack flipped the magazine shut and slammed it on the counter. With the bad PR in the paper and the problems with the new ride itself, that extra half a scream just added to his sour state of mind.

He skipped the wet suit since he didn't plan

to be out long. Maybe an hour, just to work off some of his tension. Seeing Starlight Point from the water had the same effect as seeing its lights from the darkened parking lot. He needed that perspective today.

From his house on the Old Road, Jack crossed a narrow street and walked down a small hill of sand, and then he was standing on the shores of Lake Huron.

He paddled out, far enough to come around the long break wall jutting out from the Point, and headed back along the shoreline. The Lake Breeze Hotel and its wide sand beach came into view, along with the hills of coasters crouched all over the peninsula. He stopped rowing, his kayak barely moving in the calm water.

He had enough pent-up energy to paddle all around the peninsula and across to Bayside.

But Augusta probably wouldn't be there anyway.

Jack dipped his hand in the cold water. Enough thinking of Gus. His interest in her right now was purely business. He needed to ask if she'd talk to a reporter about the Summer Training and Improvement Plan for Employees.

The wind picked up, ruffling the water. Jack started to paddle, turning his kayak and continuing down the shoreline in front of the hotel. He knew he should turn back, and he would…in just a little while, after he'd taken a look at the place where the Sea Devil got stuck last evening. Maybe if he saw it from the water, he'd get a fresh perspective.

A bald spot in the trees showed the track plainly. The exact spot where the coaster had to climb the hill using only momentum was also the only place along the shoreline unprotected from the lake wind. A strong gust blasted him from behind as he watched the Sea Devil.

A windbreak. That was the solution. Could it be as simple as that? No reengineering, no adding lifts, just a tall fence strategically placed? They could theme and paint the wall to match the ride, with swirling blue-and-white sea monsters climbing it.

Jack wanted to whoop. He wanted to let out the half a scream denied to the Sea Devil by the magazine review. He watched the ride a moment longer and then whipped his kayak around to head back down the shoreline toward home.

His joy died quickly when he saw the sky behind him.

CHAPTER FIFTEEN

STORMS ON LAKE HURON had a reputation for coming up quickly. This one outdid itself. A streak of lightning split the sky, and thunder echoed off the Lake Breeze Hotel.

The rain started almost immediately. The forecast had clearly been off by a couple of hours, and he'd been lulled into complacence. Sunshine and cloudless skies had smiled on the Point ninety percent of the summer. Until now. No way was he going out around the break wall in this storm. He'd head toward the beach and find a ride home for him and his kayak.

He beached his boat and hauled it out of the water. Keeping an eye on his kayak, Jack took shelter in the hut where guests could borrow life jackets and towels, rent floats and mini-surfboards, and buy hot dogs and drinks. He pulled his cell phone from his pocket and zipped open the plastic sandwich bag protecting it.

Mel's phone rang only once.

"Howdy, Jack."

"Where are you?"

"Hotel lobby. Flirting with a fantastic woman."

"Stay right there."

Jack debated about his kayak. Even though he owned the place, he couldn't really haul the dripping yellow boat through the lobby. He settled for leaving it with the summer employee in the rental shop.

"What name do you want to put on it?" the teenager asked. "So we know who it belongs to."

Jack grinned, not used to being anonymous at Starlight Point. He probably didn't look much like the owner in his wet T-shirt and swim trunks. No shoes.

"Jack Hamilton," he said.

"Okay," the boy replied. "I'll write it—"

Realization dawned and the teenager looked right at Jack for the first time. "Sorry, Mr. Hamilton. I didn't recognize… I mean I didn't realize—"

"It's all right." Jack smiled at the kid and

glanced at his name tag. "Mark, right? I'll be sure to ask for you when I come back later."

"I'll take good care of it."

"Thanks."

"How about a towel?" the teen offered, holding out one of the navy-and-white-striped rental towels.

"Smart idea."

The beach door of the hotel lobby opened before Jack could grab the handle. A uniformed summer employee held one half of the double door and looked him over skeptically. "Sorry, sir, you have to wear shoes inside the hotel."

"I don't have any shoes."

"Perhaps someone from your room could bring some down? I'd be glad to make a call for you." The girl was pleasant, but determined.

Now that his clothes were drenched, gooseflesh covered his exposed skin. He didn't want to stand outside his hotel and argue with one of his own employees.

He didn't have to. Mel Preston whipped open the other door and winked at the girl with a red name tag identifying her as Kris.

"Don't worry, Kris, he's with me. I'll make sure he doesn't get into any trouble."

The girl looked doubtful. "I'm supposed to enforce the shirt-and-shoes rule. I don't want to lose my job."

Gus and Evie showed up and stood just inside the door, watching the minor spectacle. Wind blew rain into the lobby.

"I'll take the fall," Mel assured the girl. His black name tag meant that he outranked her in the Starlight Point pecking order by several levels. Black tags were year-round employees, mostly management.

"Thanks," Kris said. She smiled at Jack. "Welcome to the Lake Breeze Hotel. We hope you enjoy your stay."

Jack dug his sandwich-bagged wallet out of his pocket. He gave Kris a five-dollar tip and said, "Nice job, young lady. I'll tell your supervisor you did exactly what you were supposed to do."

"Come in my bakery," Gus said. "You must be freezing. What happened?"

Jack followed her, flanked by Evie and Mel, and accepted the three small towels Gus pulled from a drawer behind the counter. He wrapped the beach towel around him and used the smaller ones to dry his head and face.

"Nothing really happened. I went for a spin with my kayak, didn't notice the storm coming up—" lightning flashed outside the windows and thunder rattled the old hotel "—and here I am."

"Where's your kayak?" Evie asked.

"Left it with a kid named Mark who works the beach shack. He'll take good care of it. The important thing," Jack said, sitting in one of the metal chairs in the bakery seating area, "is that I figured out what to do with the Sea Devil."

Mel glanced around, noted there was no one in the shop and said, "You did?"

"Uh-huh. Soon as I saw it from the water, it was obvious."

"Hit me," Mel said.

Gus placed a cup of hot coffee and a piece of warm apple pie in front of Jack. He grabbed her hand for a second before she could pull it away. "Thank you."

"That'll be five dollars," she said, smiling broadly.

"Can I have a loan? I gave my last dime

to the girl who wouldn't let me in my own hotel."

"I know," Gus said.

"The solution," Mel prompted. "I want to hear your brilliant idea."

"Windbreak. How hard would it be to put up a wall on the lower part of that hill so the train doesn't have time to slow down before it's vertical?"

Mel sat back in his chair and rubbed his chin. "Son of a chipmunk," he said. "That's the best idea I've heard all day."

"That's my big brother," Evie said. "Not just a pretty face."

"Daylight tomorrow, I'll get a crew out there to look at it. The ride designers are supposed to get here either tomorrow or Sunday, so we can run it past them, too."

Jack leaned back and half turned to face Evie, who joined him at the table, and Mel. Gus hovered behind the counter.

"Did you see the article in *Coaster Times*?" Jack asked his sister.

"Yep. Three and a half screams."

"Can you believe that? I think the Sea Devil is a solid four."

"The article was great and that's a ringing endorsement. If that doesn't make you happy," Evie said, "I don't know what you want."

Jack watched Gus as she arranged pastries in the glass case. He folded the towels methodically, never taking his eyes off her. "I guess I want to have my cake and eat it, too," he said quietly.

"Speaking of cake," Evie said cheerfully. "STRIPE starts Monday. And since it's voluntary, the audience will be a willing one."

"People wouldn't believe me when I told them it's not mandatory," Jack commented. "I had Dorothea add it to the weekly employee bulletin, and she still got a lot of calls from returning employees."

"The vendors thought I was making it up," Gus added. "But I told them it's true. I only have to teach people who want to learn."

"Who wouldn't want to learn that?" Evie asked.

Mel snorted.

Evie grinned and shook her head at Mel. "Your son must have a fifth birthday coming up this summer. Maybe a cake made by his dad would be nice."

"Of course," Mel said with only a hint of

a smile. "I'm signed up for the first night of lessons."

"Are you serious?" Jack asked.

Mel shrugged. "Since his mother pretty much skipped town, I guess it's a good thing I'm going to learn to make him a cake. Which reminds me. I was headed for the new day-care center to pick him up when you called, Jack. Can I trust your sister here to get you home safe? That is," he said, inclining his head slightly toward Gus, "unless you get a better offer."

"I'll manage. I want to stick around anyway and talk to Gus about a favor."

"Begging her for a date?" Mel whispered.

"Think I'd have a chance?"

"Maybe if you didn't smell like the lake. Good luck," Mel said, slipping out the bakery door.

"Good luck with what?" Gus asked, approaching his table.

"Everything."

"You should try making your own luck."

"I think there's a recipe for that somewhere," Evie said. "I'll go look for it." She hustled to the back room of the hotel bakery.

"That was the worst excuse imaginable

for leaving us alone," Gus said, pulling out a chair across from Jack.

"It worked, though. Augusta, there's something important I want to ask you."

"Sounds serious. Using my big-girl name and all." Gus sat on the edge of the chair, her legs turned to the side as if she was leaving herself an escape route.

Jack hesitated, wanting to reach across the table and close his hand over hers. Would she pull back? Whenever he looked at her, a spatula scooped up his heart and flipped it over in his chest.

"I need your help. I mean, Starlight Point needs your help."

"Cookie shortage somewhere?" she asked.

"Shortage of good PR. See today's paper?"

Gus nodded.

"I'm hoping you'll agree to help with a positive PR story."

"About the vendors? They," she said pointedly, "are an amazing group of people. Very dedicated to Starlight Point."

Jack's stomach sunk. "Uh, no. I mean, yes. I know they are. But the PR article we're thinking of—" he cleared his throat "—is about the STRIPE."

"Oh." Gus sat back, looking at Jack in silence.

"It was…uh…Evie's idea. Everyone likes cake. The STRIPE has a long history, so it might make a great story. And you're so beautiful you'd make us all look good." His words rushed out in one breath. He waited, eyes locked on hers. Finally, she smiled broadly, her eyes alight.

"Thank you."

"Does that mean you'll do it?" He reached across and covered her hand with his. She didn't pull away.

"Yes," she said, "but it has to be about the employees learning to make cakes, not about me. It takes more than one person to make this place a success."

"I know," Jack said. "I couldn't do it without you." When he said the words, he realized their truth. Slowly, he was starting to believe he didn't have to carry the burden of Starlight Point and its problems solely on his own shoulders. But could he risk exposing the company's secrets?

"And the other vendors," she suggested. "You need them, too."

"Yes," he admitted.

"They'd like to hear that."

"Maybe," he said, grinning. "But I'm not telling Hank and Bernie they're beautiful."

"You never know, they might like it," she said.

"Did you?"

"Of course, but the other vendors would say you're just flattering me so I'll do the article for the paper."

He blew out a breath. "You know that's not true."

The spatula flipped his heart over and squashed it flat, leaving dull anger and frustration oozing into his chest. He breathed in fresh-baked cookies and sweet frosting. Before the summer was over, the woman across from him was going to torture him to death.

Gus withdrew her hand and stood. "Maybe I only believe what I see. You spy on my meeting with the vendors and then ask me to dinner, you slam the door on my contract but then want me to be a ray of sunshine for the papers. I know it's your first year running this place, but you've got a long way to go."

She skirted the edge of the counter and disappeared into the back room, leaving Jack colder than the wet towels still draped over his shoulders. He stared at the wood grain of the table under his empty hand.

Evie appeared by his side. “Guess I’m taking you home, big brother. I’m parked behind the hotel, but you’re not allowed to drip all over my car. You can sit on the blanket in the backseat where Betty usually rides.”

Jack followed his sister through the hotel lobby in his bare feet. The incredible high of figuring out how to fix the Sea Devil had sunk to an abysmal depth. Gus had tied him to an anchor and tossed him overboard, and the worst part was that she was right. He did have a lot to learn.

Worse yet, by the time he got to his lonely house, he was going to smell like a wet dog.

CHAPTER SIXTEEN

"YOU'RE PAYING ME overtime, right?" Liz asked.

"And offering a sizable bribe," Gus said.

The two of them—along with her better summer employees and volunteers from her downtown shop—faced a group of two hundred employees assembled in the Starlight Point ballroom, ready and waiting to learn to decorate a cake.

"How the heck is this going to work?" Liz asked. "There are so many of them and only ten of us."

"Here's my plan," Gus said. "I'll do one demonstration up front. There's a camera and a big screen. Then we'll divide up. We each take twenty students to a table—Evie spent all day getting supplies at each one."

"They're not baking the actual cakes, right?" Aunt Augusta asked.

"Nope. We're providing Styrofoam circles for them to practice on."

"Whew," Liz said.

"Yep," Gus agreed. "Mrs. Hamilton took some convincing, not wanting to skimp on the details, but I finally prevailed. They *can* bake a real cake, but they don't have to."

"Mom's tough about the STRIPE," Evie said. "Always has been. The only time she had to surrender and change course was the notorious water-skiing year."

Liz laughed out loud. "What happened?"

"Use your imagination. Despite an iron will and a whole lot of faith in humanity, my mother discovered that it's *not* possible to teach everyone how to water-ski." After a moment, Evie added, "I'm glad she took the STRIPE requirement out of the contract, but I'm happy the program is still here. It's a tradition. And I think it makes her feel useful. Dad never included her much in running the park."

Virginia Hamilton made her way down the center aisle between rows of folding chairs and took the stage. Gus and her bakers in matching navy-and-white aprons stood behind the podium.

"All ready to go?" Virginia asked the crew behind her.

"Ready," Gus said. She tried to look cheerful and mighty for the good of the cause.

"Good evening," Virginia said into the handheld microphone. "Thank you for coming."

Murmuring in the audience quieted.

"As many of you know, the STRIPE is a long-standing tradition stretching back twenty-five years."

Some mumbling and whispering followed. Gus imagined people were exchanging war stories.

"This year, I'm delighted to give you the chance to learn something truly useful—how to decorate a birthday cake for someone you love."

A smattering of applause followed. Gus took this as a good sign. Teaching willing learners was a lot more fun than teaching prisoners.

"I will now turn it over to Augusta Murphy of Aunt Augusta's Bakery. Gus is a local girl who went to culinary school and the big city for a while then came home. She'll be featured in a newspaper article soon. A photographer from the paper is here tonight, and I know you'll want to be included in the feature, too, with the wonderful cakes you'll be decorating."

Gus took a deep breath then turned on her lapel mic. She stood behind a long table with bare cakes and supplies.

"Thank you, Mrs. Hamilton. Well, let's get started."

Gus placed a cake on the turntable and grabbed a pastry bag, spinning and icing while she explained. On the first cake, she piped a few simple flowers, added a border and wrote *Happy Birthday.* A photographer stood nearby and his camera flashed repeatedly during her demonstration.

"Now watch one more time while I review the steps and do another sample." The audience was dead silent. That could be good or bad, she thought. Either they were awed and enthralled or they had all fallen asleep in their hard metal chairs. She risked a glance up after she put the next cake on the turntable. All awake, all staring at her. She iced the cake, again adding flowers and a border.

"Remember, your cake doesn't necessarily have to be a birthday cake. It could be an anniversary or other holiday. As long as you have fun." She began writing as she spoke, drawing the outline of the Sea Devil and writing *Get Well Soon*. The audience laughed and the photographer snapped several pictures.

Gus looked up and saw Jack standing at the back, arms crossed over his chest. His face was invisible in the shadows, so she couldn't judge his reaction. She figured there was no harm in the joke now that Jack had discovered the solution to the ride's problems. The engineers had been there a few days ago and declared his idea a winner. Construction on the themed windbreak was already half completed, and hopes ran high for a flawless rest of the summer.

"Now," Gus said, returning her focus to the decorating class, "everyone to a practice table."

The crowd stood, bunched, shifted and moved.

Gus's table was quickly swamped. She pulled plastic tubs filled with Styrofoam circles and bags of prefilled icing from under the table, handing them out.

"Okay, step one. Let's all practice holding the pastry bag and squeezing out a row of icing. It's okay if you make a mess the first time. Everyone does."

"She's not kidding," Jack said from behind her. With his height, he looked right over her head at the circle of would-be decorators.

How was she supposed to be serious and authoritative, carrying out the STRIPE training, with a very distracting man over her shoulder? She was in charge of a cake mission here. Letting Jack mix sparkles into her batter would be a mistake.

It was bad enough that her attention followed him every time he walked past her bakery. Before or after hours, when he cruised on a junk bicycle, rubber band around his pant leg, she'd flirted with the idea of jumping on the bike and going wherever he was headed. Considering his callous treatment of the vendors and complete lack of remorse for hiking their rates, she should be considering putting a stick through his spokes and shooting him with the rubber band.

Now she was trapped, her heart fluttering like a hummingbird in a net.

"Can I join your table if I promise to listen and behave?" he asked.

She wanted to say no, but the people next to Gus moved aside, making room for Jack.

"I could send you over to Aunt Augusta's

table, but I probably ought to take pity on you. I think I saw a wooden spoon in her apron pocket. Just in case someone's not paying attention."

Jack stood right at her elbow and looked her squarely in the eye.

"You have my full attention," he whispered, a grin sliding up his face. He winked at her. Actually winked.

She glanced swiftly around the table. Everyone was either busily organizing their supplies or trying to look busy.

"You have to set a good example."

"I'll follow your every direction," he said.

Gus narrowed her eyes at him and turned to the group.

"When you pick up your bags, remember to give the top a twist before you squeeze or—"

A large plop of icing hit the table right in front of her.

"Sorry about that," Jack said.

JACK THOUGHT THE evening would never end. He'd like to spend time with Gus Murphy, but not with two hundred of his employees.

He watched Gus work the other side of the table, patiently guiding the hands of her students. He was jealous of every second she spent with someone else, a feeling he'd never experienced in the same chest-squeezing way.

He made a squiggly border around a circle on a piece of parchment paper.

"What kindergartner did that?" Mel Preston asked, grinning and pointing at Jack's attempt.

"Where'd you come from?"

"Was here all along. Jumped tables when I discovered you had the prettiest teacher."

Mel dipped his finger in Jack's icing and smeared his border.

"Hey!" Everyone stopped and stared. Jack cleared his throat. "Don't make me fire you, Mel."

Jack was aware of Gus even though she was at the other end of the table. She leaned over to help a girl direct her pastry bag. A silver *A* on a chain dangled from her neck, catching the light and riveting his attention.

Jack swallowed hard as he tried to compose his face. Gus glanced up in the sudden silence and caught him looking at her.

"Trying out for teacher's pet?" Mel asked.

"Maybe I just take cake decorating more seriously than you do."

Mel laughed, slapping Jack on the back. He pulled out his cell phone and fiddled with the buttons for a few seconds. He held the phone in Jack's face, still laughing.

"Please," Mel said, "say that again so I can record it."

"Why don't you go to another table?" Jack said.

"Maybe I better. Your sister will be nicer to me than you are. My cake will probably kick your cake's butt anyway." Mel put his phone in his pocket. "In fact, I think that's what I'll write on it."

Jack picked up his pastry bag and tried to be serious. He wanted to set a decent example. And if he happened to impress Gus Murphy in the process, it was a bonus.

Tosha Daniels, who'd been selling ice cream at the Point since Jack was a kid, was at his table. She walked over and stood just behind Gus, a finished cake in her hands. She looked at Jack without speaking.

Jack wondered just how much damage he'd done to his relationship with the vendors and if they planned to do anything about it. He hadn't heard of any more late-night meetings and no one had approached him, but no one had been friendly, either.

Except Gus.

“That looks really nice,” Jack said, pointing to Tosha’s cake. “You must be a fast learner.”

Tosha raised her eyebrows and almost smiled then stopped, her lips returning to a straight line. “Been making ice-cream cakes about as long as you’ve been alive,” she said.

Gus turned and took Tosha’s cake, exclaiming over its perfection and showing it around the table. Jack was grateful for the distraction. The mood shifted and the tension from Tosha’s set-down eased.

He concentrated on smoothing the icing on his Styrofoam circle. He made a shaky and uneven border around the top then scraped it off and tried again with slightly more success. The teenage boy next to him, who still wore his parking-attendant uniform, grinned at Jack and pointed at his shabby second try at an outline.

“Nice.”

“Thanks. I’m Jack. I’d shake hands, but I’m a sticky mess.”

“Me, too. I’m Corey.”

“Nice to meet you. You like working here?”

"So far. It's my first summer. I'm frying out there in the parking lot, dodging cars and seagulls. How long have you worked here?"

Jack laughed. "Forever."

"Why are you so dressed up?"

"Trying to make a good impression on my teacher." He watched Gus work her way around the table.

Corey looked at Jack's cake and shook his head. "Not gonna get anywhere with that." He jerked a thumb at Gus. "Maybe if you write *You're Hot* on it…"

"Good idea," Jack said, nodding slowly. "She seems like the kind of woman who would appreciate honesty. I'll consider it."

"I'm almost done," Corey said.

Jack looked at the teen's cake for the first time. Holy cow. He'd replicated the view of Starlight Point from the parking lot. There was even a tollbooth with a sign that said *Parking $8.00* and small cars in the foreground.

"How'd you do that?" Jack asked, flabbergasted.

"I like to draw. Going to art school this fall."

"What are you doing working in the parking lot? You should be drawing caricatures or working in the art department."

Corey shrugged. "That's where they put me. I'm glad to have a job. Gotta save up for school."

Gus now stood next to Corey, enthralled with his cake.

"Come see me tomorrow morning and we'll talk about finding you a better job."

"Where do you work?"

"Office building up front. Ask for Jack Hamilton."

"Doesn't he own the place?"

"I sure do."

"Sorry, Jack," Gus said. "This young man is going to be working for me tomorrow."

Jack stood and went nose to nose with Gus. "I saw him first."

Gus laughed. "I hate giving in, but I'll let you win this time." She picked up Corey's artwork on the Styrofoam circle. "But I hope you'll let me use this as an example." She patted Corey's shoulder. "This is amazing work."

"Just the view I see every day," he said.

"It's my favorite view of Starlight Point," Gus said, "except I like it at night with a midnight-blue sky behind the white lights of the rides."

Jack couldn't believe his ears. That was his view. The view of Starlight Point he'd carried since he was young enough to ride in his mother's wagon. The view he saw when he closed his eyes, even on the hottest, brightest day of July.

He was speechless.

Corey said goodbye and left. Gus glanced up at Jack, who was staring at her. And trying not to kiss her in front of everyone.

"What?" she asked. Her green gaze searched his, and he was afraid to think of what his eyes gave away.

"What are you doing after class tonight?" he asked.

"Cleaning up," she said, sweeping a hand at the ten tables covered with icing and surrounded by people still working on their cakes. "And then collapsing. We have to do this all over again tomorrow and then a few nights next week for anyone else who wants to give it a try."

The magnitude of the project hit Jack.

"Are we paying you?" he asked.

Gus's expressive eyes turned to stone.

"Virginia has offered to pay for all the supplies and the hourly wage of my employees."

"What about you?"

"I'm not hourly."

"But this is taking up your time, and I know you're busy. I've seen all the early mornings and late nights you've been here."

"You have?"

Jack nodded.

They were still nose to nose. Jack nearly forgot the hundred or so other people in the room, some of them only feet away at their table. He focused on Augusta. He leaned a little closer. She mirrored his action. Then swayed back abruptly.

"I…um…like teaching people to do something I love," she said. "So it's not all work and no pay. You never know when you might find a great talent who'll come work for you later."

"As long as you grab the talent fast," Jack said.

"Got me there."

Jack took Gus's hand, not caring that his was sticky or that people were watching.

"Let me help you," he said.

"Don't tempt me. I need someone to clean

two hundred sticky pastry bags and scrape icing off the ballroom floor."

"Since I made part of the mess, I should help clean it up."

"True."

"That was the STRIPE topic the summer I was twelve. Civility and good manners. I would be glad to hold the door for you or fold napkins into swans anytime."

Gus shook her head. "You're a complicated man, Jack Hamilton, but I'll take you up on your offer."

"Holding the door or folding the swans?"

"Cleaning the floor."

GUS WANTED TO tell Jack to go home. It was late. Her baking recruits had left half an hour ago, leaving the rest of the cleanup to a crew Virginia had scheduled. They were in the ballroom kitchen, clouds of steam rising over the sinks where they washed icing bags and pastry tips.

Jack used a wide broom, pushing it up and down the long rows on the wood ballroom floor. His white shirtsleeves were rolled above the elbow, shirttail hanging out in the back. No jacket or tie. He handled the broom smoothly, flipping it around at the end of each swath.

"I'm guessing you've done that before," Gus said, leaning against the back wall.

Jack reached the end of a row near her and stopped. "Ten-year-olds will do anything for a dollar. Used to sweep this floor and the hotel lobby." He grinned. "I thought I was the luckiest kid in town. Got paid a buck every day. By the end of the summer, I had enough for a new bike."

"I used to wash Aunt Augusta's cake pans and pastry bags for a dollar. Bought a little cash register and pink oven with my earnings. I had quite a business selling cupcakes to my friends at school until the lunch ladies shut me down. They didn't like competition."

Jack laughed. "And now look at us. You own a bakery, and I'm still sweeping the floors."

"I hope you're making more than a dollar."

Jack's grin faded. He cupped his hands over the end of the broom handle and rested his chin on his hands. "Honestly, I'm not sure I'm even making that."

Gus crossed her arms over her chest. "Sure you are. I'm making decent money here, and you'll be getting twenty percent of it." *Ouch,* she thought, *that didn't sound very friendly even though it's true.*

Jack lowered his eyes, nudging the bottom of the broom with his toe.

"When you get my June payment, you'll cheer up," she said, trying for a light tone. "Might even be able to get yourself a new bike instead of that old tandem one you ride."

Jack still said nothing, looking at the floor.

"You look pretty lonely on that bike," Gus said, her voice soft. His silence drove her nuts. Why didn't he spar with her as usual? She glanced around the empty ballroom, desperate to smooth the rough edge between them. "I'd ask you to dance, but I don't think I could compete with your current partner. You and that broom move together like old friends."

Finally. A smile. Jack shook out the broom and leaned it against the wall next to Gus.

"Take a walk with me on the beach?" he asked.

She wanted to say yes. She wanted to ask him why dark clouds hovered between them whenever business entered the conversation.

"Maybe as far as the parking lot," she said.

"I'll take it."

Jack used his key to open a gate right behind the ballroom. Starlight Point was surrounded by gates, most of them leading to the Outer Loop, some of them straight to the beach.

"You might want to take your shoes off," Jack said, his voice clear in the night air.

Gus stepped right onto the sand.

"I was thinking of the boardwalk when I agreed to this," she said.

"Not on this part of the Point. There's another gate leading into the lot where your van's parked, but it's all sandy beach between here and there." He reached down and pulled off his shoes, stuffed his socks into his suit-coat pocket and held both shoes in the hand farthest away from Gus. "It's a solitary stretch."

"Won't Security wonder what we're doing out here?"

"No late-night security in this part of the park."

"Living dangerously," she said.

"I hope not."

Gus kicked off her shoes and picked them up. Without thinking, she reached for Jack's hand. The sand under her feet was cool now in the darkness. She shivered a little.

"Want my coat?' Jack asked.

"I'm all right. It's not far to the lot."

Sand slipped under their feet. The soft sound of waves brushed the shore.

"Is this summer turning out like you thought?" Jack asked.

She considered that question for a moment. The short answer was yes, most of it.

"I expected to be baking like crazy and I thought I might get some sun. I hoped it would be fun on occasion."

"And?"

"Yes to two of those. I'm not out in the sun very much because I'm inside baking."

"But you are having fun?" he asked.

"I am right now. I'm walking the moonlit beach with someone who..." She stopped, shocked by how close she'd come to saying something she'd hardly admitted to herself.

Jack stepped in front of her, dropping his shoes with a soft clunk on the sand. "Someone who what?"

She let go of her shoes and used her free hand to rake her fingers through her hair. How was she going to answer his question?

The truth? Someone who got under her skin. Someone she looked for around every corner. Someone she wanted to kiss her right now. And the next day.

"Someone..."

Jack stepped closer, the tension between them like the moment at the top of a roller-coaster hill. Suspended, waiting, thrilling.

"If I were going to finish that sentence," he said, "I'd say I was walking the moonlit beach with someone who always leaves me wanting more."

Gus tried to still the fluttering just under her collarbones. She couldn't argue with Jack. She knew she left him wanting more. She left herself wanting more. There was a reason she rode the coaster to the top of the hill but hesitated, afraid to go over. She repeated her mantra to herself. She was a vendor. Jack had mistreated the vendors. He'd shown no remorse. She owed Tosha, and Bernie...

The reasons were like elastic stretched too far, getting thinner and thinner. Jack tested all her powers of resistance. If she coasted over the hill with him, there would be no going back. Too much depended on her having a successful summer to risk her heart and everything else.

She picked up her shoes. “Maybe you should show me that gate to the parking lot.”

CHAPTER SEVENTEEN

THREE NIGHTS LATER, Augusta rolled out of bed and pulled on yoga pants, a lightweight sweatshirt and sneakers. It was no use trying to sleep when all she could think about was fire consuming the Last Chance Bakery and the rest of the Wonderful West.

And it would be all her fault for leaving that oven on.

She'd been up since midnight, when she was jolted awake by the sensation that she'd forgotten something. She'd tried to rationalize—the ovens ran almost twelve hours a day without burning down the kitchen. Was running twelve hours overnight any different?

It was no use.

The clock in her van read 1:03 a.m. when she pulled out of the lot behind her downtown bakery. The lone guard in the tollbooth at the entrance of Starlight Point waved her through. Evidently he wasn't curious as to why she was passing through the gates nine hours before the park opened.

Gus cut across the empty front lot to the Outer Loop. There wasn't a person or vehicle in sight.

Her headlights illuminated the gate providing closest access to the Last Chance Bakery. She left the van running, lights on, as she opened the gate. It should take five minutes to dash past the Western-themed carousel, check her oven and be back in the van heading home for a few more hours of sleep.

The lights that illuminated the walkways and rides during operating hours were out. Heavy darkness made the familiar buildings seem like strangers looming in the night. Gus hurried past the horses on the silent merry-go-round.

She'd almost made it to her bakery when she heard sounds coming from the shooting gallery and arcade. Change jingling and hushed voices. She stopped, and a cold thrill of nerves raced through her.

Could it be maintenance cleaning or servicing the games? Not likely. They would turn the lights on if they were working in the old arcade. The flickers of light she saw were from flashlights. They almost looked like yellow flames lapping up the darkness. The thought reminded her of the bakery, the reason she was there.

She longed to forget the arcade, check on the Last Chance and get back across the Point Bridge. However, a nagging sense of loyalty to Starlight Point wouldn't let her ignore the strange sounds. She touched the cell phone in the front pocket of her sweatshirt. Who would she call? Everyone was asleep. She wasn't going to wake Jack or Evie just on a suspicion.

She stepped onto the front porch of the arcade, and the old wood boards let out a squeak that cut the night. Amid the music and laughter of park guests, no one would've noticed. But in the deserted park, the sound was a doorbell announcing her presence.

The flashlights switched off. Gus held her breath for a second, waiting. Suddenly, the door crashed open and two men barreled into her. In a flash, she recognized the one in front, a teenager who had worked in the arcade earlier that summer until he was fired for theft. She'd been there the day security escorted him past her Last Chance bakery.

She didn't see the second man's face because the first one shoved her backward. She tried to catch herself, but her head struck a post supporting the porch roof and the dark night became even blacker as she fell to the cracked concrete walkway.

JACK'S CELL PHONE woke him up from a deep sleep. Instinctively, he grabbed the phone and glanced at the time. Who the heck would be calling him at one thirty in the morning?

He swiped the screen and mumbled a confused hello.

"Bayside Police dispatch. Is this Jack Hamilton?"

He didn't recognize the dispatcher's detached voice, but she had his full attention anyway.

"Yes. What's wrong?"

"Report of a robbery in progress at Starlight Point. We're sending officers and an ambulance."

"What?" He jumped out of bed and stepped into jeans and sneakers from the pile on his bedroom floor. Shirtless, he moved toward the kitchen, where his keys hung on a hook by the door.

"A woman called it in. Said two men were robbing the arcade in the Wonderful West. They attacked her and took off."

A chill racked Jack's body. Cell phone still at his ear, he was already opening his car door.

"Who reported it?"

"A woman named—" the dispatcher paused as if consulting her notes "—Augusta Murphy."

As Jack sped across the lot, his heart raced like an overworked engine. Questions tortured him. What was Augusta doing at the park in the middle of the night? She wouldn't be baking at this hour. Would she? Was she hurt? Where were the robbers now?

The flashing lights on three police cars and an ambulance approached from the Point Bridge on his left and he slowed to let them onto the Outer Loop ahead of him.

They were the real heroes here.

He was the fool who'd cut security, shut off lights and exposed Starlight Point to this kind of situation.

Worse than that, he'd put someone he cared about in danger. All he could see was Augusta's beautiful face and open smile. Was she injured? How badly? He tried to calm his panicked thoughts by remembering that she had called in the burglary. Even if she needed an ambulance, even if she had been attacked, she was still able to make a phone call.

He followed the rescue squad to the gate where the nighttime security guard waited, headlights illuminating the area. The tollbooth was now unmanned, but the worst was already happening so it didn't matter. Also at the gate, Gus's pink delivery van sat, still running, headlights on. The sight of her vehicle made the danger more real—there was no doubting who had called in the burglary now. Who had been attacked.

Jack got out of his car, cursing himself for every stupid decision he'd made that summer. He switched off her van as he went by.

At least the burglars hadn't stolen it. But what else had they done? He would hand over the keys to Starlight Point if it would mean Augusta was unharmed.

Guns drawn, the Bayside police went through the gate first. Jack followed too closely, focused on finding Gus.

Where is she?

They passed the carousel, a shuttered hotdog stand, the empty queue lines for a family ride. Moving slowly, flashlights sweeping the area. Too slowly.

"The arcade is right here," Jack said.

The lights were out and the door stood open like an empty mouth. Still no Augusta. But a light was on in the back of her bakery only two buildings away.

Jack tapped the cop on the shoulder and indicated the light. He and one officer headed for the Last Chance Bakery while the others searched the arcade.

The front door was locked when the police officer stealthily turned the handle.

"Never know if the robbers are in there or if they've got her hostage," he whispered.

The thought of Augusta being held hostage removed any trace of calmness Jack had tried to hang on to. He dashed around to the back and used his height to peer in a high window usually left open for ventilation.

The only thing he saw was Gus. On the floor. Covered in blood. He jerked on the door handle, but it was locked.

"Augusta, it's me. Jack," he yelled. He returned to the window and finally breathed when he saw her get up and move slowly toward the door.

She'd only opened it an inch when he squeezed through and pulled her against him. She sagged in his arms. The police officer swept the bakery quickly and declared it clear. He left, promising to return with the paramedics.

"Sit down, Gus," Jack said, reluctant to release her but desperate to assess her condition.

"No chairs," she mumbled.

"Don't you ever sit down at the bakery?"

"Not enough room."

"Remind me to build an addition. Tomorrow." He picked Augusta up and set her on the counter so her face was level with his. With relief, he quickly saw where most of the blood was coming from. A cut under her hair still oozed bright red.

Jack grabbed paper towels from the wall dispenser by the sink, ran them under cold water and applied pressure. He had never seen Augusta so quiet.

"Where else are you hurt?"

"Nowhere. Just scrapes." She held up her elbow for him to see where she'd hit the pavement.

With one hand holding the towels on her head, he held her close with the other arm. He had never taken the time to put on a shirt, and Gus's eyelashes brushed against his bare chest when she blinked.

"I'm so sorry," he whispered.

"Not your fault."

"Yes, it is."

"You didn't knock me over running from a robbery."

"I cut security down to nothing. That was my decision. My responsibility," he said.

The paramedics, an older man and a young woman, came through the back door and peeled Augusta out of Jack's arms. They placed her on the gurney and assessed her with professional precision. After applying a bandage and instant ice pack to her head, they asked her a dozen questions to evaluate the severity of her head injury. She answered with the date, time, her name, occupation, the name of the current president and her birth date.

"Were you working late tonight…or early?" the young woman asked.

Gus smiled faintly. "Neither. I came in to check an oven. Didn't want to burn down Starlight Point," she said.

"Was the oven on when you got here?" Jack asked.

"No. Stone cold. All this for nothing."

Jack took one of her hands and held it.

"We're going to take you to the hospital for X-rays and evaluation," the older paramedic said. "And you'll need a few stitches."

Gus held up her free hand. "Not necessary. I feel better. I can drive myself."

"You're not driving yourself," Jack said.

"I don't need an ambulance. Really."

"I'll take you." Jack looked to the paramedics for approval.

"Are you a relative?"

"No. I own this place and I'm responsible for what happens to everyone here. And I'm…a friend."

The man shrugged. "Sign here and you can take the liability for her."

Jack kept her hand in his. "I'll take *care* of her," he said, watching her expression and hoping she would let him.

Gus didn't protest. "Can we take my van? I can't leave it here."

"Of course. But you'll have to let me drive."

The chief of the Starlight Point police department barged through the back door. "Caught two teenagers walking the beach around the peninsula. Bayside police got 'em in a squad car. They're bringing them around for you to identify."

Gus paled and Jack tightened his grip on her hand. "You don't have to do this," he said.

"I can tell you who one of them is. He worked in the arcade the first few weeks of the season, but I heard he got fired for stealing," Augusta said. "Stocky kid, messy blond hair."

"I can ID that one," the chief said. "Open-and-shut case. And the kid with him should probably learn to keep better company. Now they've got breaking and entering, robbery and assault on their records."

"Not assault," Gus said. "They pushed me over and ran. Scared, stupid kids. If they'd really meant to hurt me..." Her words trailed off, but the knot in Jack's gut tightened.

"You take over tonight," he told his chief of security. "Drive my car to my office and leave it there. Keys are in it. We're having a meeting tomorrow to review our security policy. What happened tonight will never happen again."

Jack slowly pulled Gus to her feet and walked her to the van someone had driven in from the gate. He buckled her in and got in the driver's seat.

The fact that his cost cutting had endangered Augusta tore him to pieces. He had to save Starlight Point, but he couldn't do it by hurting the people he loved.

OVER THE NEXT two days, Gus had more visitors to her third-floor apartment than she'd seen in the almost ten months she'd lived there.

Evie came by twice and called several more times to report that the bakeries at the Point were surviving. The talented teenager who'd been stuck on parking-lot duty was reassigned to work in her midway bakery and his decorating skills were quickly drawing attention. According to Evie, Jack had walked Corey to the bakery and handed him an apron.

Gus was anxious to get back to her bakeries, but the doctor had insisted she take some time off. Aunt Augusta's fussing—she hadn't left Gus's bedside since Jack reluctantly drove away the morning after the robbery—was driving her crazy, no matter how well-intentioned. She'd finally gotten her aunt to go back to work by telling her she'd rest easier knowing the downtown shop was in good hands. Aunt Augusta had even called Gus's parents in China to tell them what happened and assure them their daughter was in good hands. Gus rolled her eyes during the first part of the phone conversation and then insisted on talking to them herself so they wouldn't think she'd lost an eye or something.

Being babied was not in Gus's repertoire. She wanted to grab an apron and frost something. Anything.

During the afternoon lull at the Point, several of her vendor friends came across on the ferry to bring her a hot dog and fries. "Wanted to bring you an ice-cream cake," Tosha said, "but I didn't think it would hold up. Hot out there."

"We got you these," Bernie said, holding out a bunch of flowers.

Tosha set them on a table by the window, beside a vase filled with a dozen pink roses.

"Secret admirer?" she asked.

"They're from Jack Hamilton," Gus answered. There was no point denying it when Tosha could easily see the card for herself. He hadn't written a gushy message. Just an honest one.

I'm so sorry this happened. I hope you feel better soon. Jack.

"Sounds like he feels guilty for chopping security," Tosha said. "He should."

"Maybe," Gus said. "But it's not his fault I thought I left an oven on and was roaming around in the middle of the night."

"I heard he beefed up security around the clock since the robbery," Bernie said. "Back to the way his father had it. Maybe that boy is learning."

Gus still had a headache and didn't feel like defending Jack or arguing with her friends. They talked about neutral topics, assured her they were looking out for her bakeries until she got back on her feet, hugged her and left.

The next day was a disaster waiting to happen. A three-tiered wedding cake and five sheet cakes for extra servings had to be delivered. The bakery staff would decorate the cakes—and Augusta had no doubts about her aunt's skills. After all, Gus had learned from her aunt. She was worried about who would drive the big pink van. Since she'd bought it, none of the ladies in her shop had volunteered to get behind the wheel.

Her doorbell rang at eight o'clock Saturday morning. Gus pulled the front curtain aside and looked through the narrow window. Jack stood wearing a bright pink T-shirt with her company logo. She opened the door.

Jack pulled her into a hug. "Let me see you," he said, drawing back her hair and taking a close look at her stitches. He kissed her temple. "I hope you got my flowers."

"I did…thank you," Gus said.

"I wish I could stay, but I'm on a mission. I need the keys to the cake wagon."

"Why?"

"It matches my shirt."

"Did my aunt rope you into delivering a wedding cake today?"

"*Rope*," Jack said, "is not the word. I offered to help out in any way possible, and I got the job of driving the heavy machinery because I'm the man."

"Want me to come along?"

Jack kissed her other temple. "No. Your job is to rest. One more day. Aunt Augusta and I have this under control."

"But it's Saturday, the busiest day at the Point."

"That's why I have all those excellent employees. Besides, I left Evie in charge. I'm not worried."

CHAPTER EIGHTEEN

"THANK GOODNESS YOUR stitches are finally out and those stupid cake classes are over," Evie said. "The last ten days have been purgatory."

"The STRIPE classes were a pain," Gus said, "but now I'm a little sad. What will I do with those extra twenty hours this week?"

Evie laughed. "What's my brother going to do every night? I'm not the only one who noticed he showed up to every class."

"He takes cake seriously. Or he could be setting a great example for your summer employees."

"Right."

Gus frowned and shook her head slowly. "Evie, I'm sorry to tell you this, but I think your brother may be a—" she paused, looking around dramatically and continuing in a whisper "—slow learner."

Evie chuckled. "Give me a break. You know as well as I do why he was there."

"I do. He felt guilty taking up my valuable baking time and offered to help out. He scrubbed that ballroom floor icing-free every night."

"I thought he stayed for a chance to be alone with you," Evie said.

"Just once."

"And?"

"A short walk on the beach. No more," Gus said.

"If I know my brother, I'd say he wants more."

"That's what he said."

"So?"

"Complications. We're not exactly in the same pay grade here," Gus said. "Besides, that was before the whole robbery, getting-whacked-on-the-head incident. Things are… different between us now."

"Hmm."

"And it's a long summer. I'm taking things one bite at a time right now."

Evie saved her file and closed the laptop, giving her full attention to Gus, who was busy icing red, white and blue cookies. The Fourth of July, the midpoint of summer, was only one day away.

"Are you staying for the fireworks tomorrow night?"

"Uh-huh," Gus said. "I hear it's a show that rivals Disneyland. Gotta see that. Although I heard the traffic across the Point Bridge is such a snarl that you might as well hang out here after. Maybe I'll stay all night and get the next morning's baking done early."

"Employees don't play in the holiday traffic. We party in the staff parking lot. Except the kids with curfews take the ferry to downtown Bayside."

"Parking-lot party?" Gus asked. It sounded illegal. But tempting.

"You have to experience it. Trunks filled with drinks on ice, folding chairs, a portable fire pit. One year we even had a band from the live shows. No rules. Zero chance of sunburn."

"And this goes on all night?" Gus asked.

"Yes."

"And security looks the other way?"

"Only long enough to get something out of their coolers. And they usually come to the party late along with the kids who direct traffic. Either way, it's better than sitting on the Point Bridge in a tangle of tourists."

Gus finished putting glitter sprinkles on a fireworks cookie. "Sounds like good time management to me. Party until the traffic clears."

"Or until everyone gets tired. Or pairs off."

Gus looked at Evie and raised her eyebrows.

"Not necessarily speaking from experience," Evie said. "But Starlight Point is no stranger to summer romances. You should get in on the action."

"I'll consider it. But I'd have to leave before dawn. Baker's curse."

"You wouldn't be alone. A little parade of employee cars files out of the lot just before the sun comes up," Evie said. "I'm lucky. I can just walk home across the parking lot."

Gus grinned at the usually straight-laced girl.

"Does Jack know about this?"

"He walks home, too."

"Interesting."

"Name tags are off at the party and everyone just has fun. We call it Midsummer Madness because anything can happen."

"I don't think I—"

"Don't say no, Gus. You need to have some fun with the rest of us."

"What I was going to say is I don't think I

have a large enough cooler for a huge van like mine. People will have expectations based on relative size. And boy am I going to be conspicuous rolling out of here in the early-morning July-fifth parade."

JACK STOOD IN the back door of the Midway Bakery until Gus noticed him. She was busy. A long line stretched in front of her bakery and her apron was smeared with icing. A streak of white flour highlighted her cheekbone. Usually neat and in control, she whirled from oven to counter with a tray in each hand. A chunk of long brown hair escaped her hat and she shoved it back with an oven-mitted hand—probably the reason for the flour on her cheek.

One summer when he was seventeen and running the brake on the Silver Streak, he'd been infatuated with a girl who worked at the guessing booth nearby. All season long, he'd heard her over the microphone guessing ages and weights. Adored her as she handed out stuffed animals and other prizes. All the while willing her to notice the quiet boy with a red name tag that said Jack. She never did.

Since then, he'd steered clear of summer romances, always using the excuse that he was too busy. His real reason, though, was that he'd never encountered a woman who could compete with his love for Starlight Point.

Until now. Gus finally acknowledged him with a look. She must have seen him standing there at least two minutes earlier, but she'd made him wait. He didn't mind. It gave him time to watch her.

"Just a minute," she said. She took a tray of iced cookies up front, where four summer employees rang up sales like traders on the floor of the New York Stock Exchange.

"Five minutes of your time?" he asked when she came back. He pulled two cold bottles of soda out of a bag.

She smiled. "For one of those, I'd give you ten."

She stepped past him to the outdoor break area. A few employees sat at the far end of a picnic table, a boy and a girl who saw only each other.

It was punishingly hot. Jack took off his suit jacket and tossed it on an empty table. He dragged the table into the small ring of shade created by the overhangs from the surrounding shops.

"Sit down and cool off," he said.

"You can't imagine how wonderful that sounds." She sat on a bench under the shady overhang. He slid in right next to her.

"I could try. We have a record crowd today. I was just up front looking at gate receipts. Could be thirty thousand here."

"I'm pretty sure I've made that many cookies today. And cupcakes. Red, white and blue frosting will be in my dreams tonight."

"Sounds like a great dream to me."

Gus grinned at him. "Sweet tooth," she said.

"How is your head?"

"Fine. All better. Stitches out two days ago, and no one will ever see the scar under my hair."

"I'll know it's there," Jack said. "I can't forget what happened to you."

"I forgave you after you drove my aunt and eight cakes in the pink van. You could give yourself a break."

"I'll try to do that right now." Jack leaned against the wall and sipped his drink. Even in the shade, coat off, cold drink in hand, there was zero chance of cooling down when Gus's shoulder brushed his every time she lifted the bottle to her lips. And he couldn't take his eyes off her lips.

"Great weather for fireworks later," Jack commented. "I hear you're staying to watch."

Gus raised an eyebrow and leaned against the wall next to Jack.

"Evie told me," he said.

"Thought so."

"Have you ever seen our fireworks show?"

She nodded. "A few times when I was younger. But not from here at the Point. I watched from downtown Bayside with my parents and Aunt Augusta."

"It's better here. We have timed music. And thirty thousand sweaty people jostling for the good viewing places."

"A deal I can't refuse." She turned toward him, leaning a little closer. "You have inside knowledge. Where can I get the best view?"

"Actually, that's why I came by." Before he lost his nerve, he had to ask her. "Will you watch the fireworks with me tonight?"

He put his hand over hers. She didn't pull away but glanced down at their joined hands on the splintered surface of the bench. He had to fill the silence before she said no.

"We usually watch from the Star Spiral.

When you're up two hundred feet, the fireworks explode almost right in front of you."

Gus put her free hand over top of his and leaned closer.

This was encouraging. "Say you'll watch the show with me tonight," he said.

"I will," she said quickly and then jumped up and disappeared into her bakery.

Jack stood in the shade for a second, wondering if his mother and sister would mind watching the fireworks somewhere else tonight. It would break tradition, but that was the story of this whole summer.

CHAPTER NINETEEN

GUS LEFT HER employees in charge, with plenty of change in the cash register and a display case full of cookies and cupcakes.

She walked to the employee center, which was partly hidden by a stand of tall trees. The building had showers and change rooms, a cheap cafeteria, employee wardrobe and uniform counter, mail service, and a small rec room and lounge.

She eyed the jeans and T-shirt she'd changed into and wished for something better. For all she knew, Jack would still be wearing a suit and she'd step into a party at the Star Spiral with a host of invited guests. With champagne, party favors and flashy jewelry. How many people did Jack mean when he said "we" watch from there?

"Wow. I don't usually see you without an apron," Evie said. She was at the counter getting the special of the day—hot dog and fries on a red, white and blue plate.

"I'm taking the night off."

"I know. I'm watching the fireworks from the upper hotel balcony tonight," Evie said.

"I thought you'd be at the Star Spiral."

"Not this year. Mom and I decided to do something different."

Evie grinned at Gus and turned back to the food counter.

You shouldn't be nervous, Gus told herself as she walked through the gate. The beach path was a safe way to avoid crowds on busy days. And this was a busy day. Jack's guess at thirty thousand had seemed impossible, but as more people passed her shop she started to believe it. The sheer volume of cookies and cupcakes sold was keeping all her employees busy and had prompted three phone calls to Evie to suggest upping their supply order for the coming week.

Gus stopped and leaned on the rail, watching the pinks and oranges of the sunset fading and skimming across the water. She thought about Jack. They'd been fencing since they met. Masks on, swords up, doing a slow dance in a circle. And for what?

He was available.

She was available.

But she was thirty thousand dollars deeper in debt because of his changes to his father's contracts. She shouldn't be meeting him at the Star Spiral. Maybe she could honor her commitment to the other vendors and try to negotiate with him during the fireworks. Patriotic fervor might inspire his generosity.

Who am I kidding? She watched the dozens of boats anchored in the lake, their green and red lights bobbing as the sun sunk lower. The boaters would have a great view of the fireworks tonight. And so would she.

She dug her employee identification from her jeans pocket, passed through the beach gate and walked purposefully through the crowd toward the Star Spiral.

The base of the ride was empty, deserted. Walled in by other rides and buildings, the area around the loading platform would make a disappointing viewing spot for the fireworks.

Gus remembered the exhilaration of riding the Star Spiral when she was very young. The round glass cabin rose slowly, spinning almost imperceptibly, until it suddenly broke over the tops of all the surrounding buildings. It rose smoothly up the shaft to a height of two hundred feet and spun several times. The panoramic view of Starlight Point's peninsula and the lake and bay was spectacular. She remembered standing with her nose and toes to the glass and the feeling of falling as the cabin slowly descended.

That same feeling whooshed through her chest every time she saw Jack or thought of him.

One lonely employee was in the operator's hut. Gus waved and walked straight to the circular ramp to enter the ride. Jack stood at the turnstile. He wore loose-fitting jeans and a gray Starlight Point T-shirt. The shadows almost concealed his identity, but his height and muscular physique were unmistakable. If not for the turnstile, Gus would have walked straight into Jack's arms, drawn by the force of her feelings.

The silver metal clunked around and swatted her in the butt, sending her a hopping step into Jack. Ungraceful, but effective. The distance between them snapped shut.

"Are you waiting here to greet all your guests?" She glanced at the windows of the ride cabin, but no one was visible behind the dark glass.

"Everyone I invited is here," he said. He draped an arm around her and walked her up the slanted entrance. Inside the cabin, Jack pulled the door shut and latched it.

"Are you sure you know what you're doing?" Gus asked.

"With the ride?"

Gus swallowed and bit her lip. "Uh-huh."

"Worked this ride one summer," he said. "Today Ben is operating it from down there."

"I'm not sure I know what *I'm* doing."

"Watching the fireworks."

"I mean alone. With you," she said.

"Am I that bad to be around?"

She shook her head. *That good*, she thought. "You test my loyalty."

The ride lurched into a slow spin, and Gus swayed with the sudden movement. Jack reached for her and pulled her into his arms. "You test my self-control," he murmured against her ear, "because whenever I see you, I want to do this."

His lips grazed her ear, then moved across her cheek and found her mouth. The kiss was soft, sweet, a longer taste of their first kiss, in his car outside her loft. She wanted it to go on all night.

A ripple of excitement lapped through her—like the feeling of walking far out into the water and no longer touching bottom so you have to start swimming. This was a leap of faith just like that.

Color and noise exploded around them, startling her into pulling back.

"Just fireworks," he said. They stood in front of a bank of windows in each other's arms, suspended above a crowd of thousands with fireworks coloring the air right in front of them. The magic of his touch and his kiss was multiplied by every sparkling explosion.

"How long does it last?" Gus whispered. She wasn't sure if she meant the fireworks or the delicious feeling of being alone with a man she couldn't resist, but couldn't possess. Or could she? So what if they worked together. Aunt Augusta had said many local couples met at Starlight Point. Why couldn't she have a romance here, too?

She knew the reason. But her loyalty to the vendors and her frustration over his close-mouthed cost cutting felt like a flimsy excuse to back away from a man who ignited her senses. At least it did right now. She might see this differently by daylight instead of starlight.

Jack furrowed his brow and appeared puzzled as he considered her question, although it might have been the collection of colors reflected through the glass. Perhaps he was as confused as she was.

"The fireworks show," Gus explained.

"Oh." Jack visibly tried to focus. "Five minutes."

Gus laughed. "Five minutes?"

He nodded. Swallowed hard.

"I've seen better shows at the county fair. It must be longer than that," she said.

He dropped his arms and turned so they were no longer touching. They stood side by side at the glass.

"Best I could do this year," he said.

Gus was silent, wondering what went on behind the closed door of his office.

"I had to shave costs," he continued. "Wish I hadn't now…for two reasons. I could stay up here all night, watching the fireworks with you."

"You own the place. You can do whatever you want."

Jack didn't respond, just continued watching the fireworks.

"And your other reason?"

"Huge crowd. I feel like I owe them more. They're definitely going to notice it's a short show this year. People will talk. Wish I'd thought about that."

"So why did you cut it back so much?"

He returned his attention to Gus. "Do you know five minutes of high-quality fireworks and pyrotechnics—the kind people expect from Starlight Point—is thirty thousand dollars? Or even more depending on what you get and how far you space them apart. Thirty thousand bucks is a lot of money for a few minutes." He let out a long, slow breath and crossed his arms over his chest. "But I regret this decision anyway."

She didn't want to say it. Did not want to kick him while he was down. But there it was. Thirty thousand dollars. The same amount he'd robbed her of this summer. And she wasn't the only one. This was why he tested her loyalty. She wondered if he regretted changing the vendor contracts as much as the decision to chop the Fourth of July show.

Jack's jaw was tight as he watched the

streaks of red, white and blue fade. If he would only admit it. Say he'd treated her and the other vendors badly. Why couldn't he? Was it so hard to let his guard down and open up?

They stood shoulder to shoulder like casual acquaintances and watched the fireworks light the roller coasters, the bright white facade of the hotel and the midway lined with thousands of people.

The grand finale exploded over Starlight Point. It was only thirty seconds long and seemed like a tiny, disappointing dessert to a sparse meal. Jack was right about one thing: people would certainly notice the skimpy fireworks display. Gus decided it was time for some raw honesty.

"So," she said carefully. "Short fireworks show, short staffing on the nighttime crews and shortchanging your vendors. You're having quite a summer. What do you plan to do with all the cash you save?"

"You don't know what you're talking about."

"So enlighten me."

"I can't."

The Star Spiral started turning and making its slow descent. They had only fifteen seconds or so of privacy left.

"You can kiss me, eat my cookies and drive me crazy all summer, but you can't tell me what kind of financial scheme you're running?"

"It's not a scheme."

Gus backed away and sat down on the bench that circled the central shaft of the Star Spiral. She felt a little queasy now that the fireworks were over, the ride was in motion and her relationship with Jack was a high-speed roller coaster.

The ride stopped. Jack opened the door but paused, one hand on the handle.

"Do I really drive you crazy?" he asked.

Exasperated, Gus cocked her head to one side and gave him a look that answered the question.

"Good," he said, his voice once again soft. "Because you've got me completely insane. It may not be obvious to you right now, but this was the best ride I've had at Starlight Point in a long time."

Gus thought he'd walk away and avoid her the rest of the summer.

But he did the unexpected.

He took her hand, walked through the door and waved curtly to Ben at the operator's perch. Gus wondered what the teenager thought about their private ride and considered sending him some baked goods so he'd keep quiet about this particular spin on the Star Spiral.

Jack was headed for the party in the employee parking lot right outside the front gate. He held her hand and showed no signs of slowing down. She *could* jerk out of his grasp and run the other direction. She *could* try to use darkness as a cover. Not that she was ashamed to be with Jack. Any woman would want to be in her shoes right now. She risked a glance at his tall frame. Handsome. Smart. Successful. Dedicated to his work and his family. And he had a sweet tooth. He appreciated her line of work.

But there was an obvious problem.

And it was right in front of her, in the employee lot. Hank's hot-dog wagon was parked beside Bernie's Boardwalk Fries van. In the mix of people moving though the headlights, Gus made out another half a dozen vendors. They appeared to have their own area of the parking lot. And she'd have to walk right through it with Jack's hand in hers if she wanted to get to the other side of the lot where her pink van sat amid a group of cars, lanterns, folding chairs and moving people.

She stopped.

"What is it?" Jack asked. "I see your van right over there. Evie and company are probably waiting for us."

Gus said nothing, staring at the group of vendors who'd already noticed her. "See," Jack said, tugging her hand a little. "Right over there."

"I see it. I just want to say hello to some people before I go over there."

Jack shrugged. "Okay with me. We've got all night."

Tosha and Ricardo handed out cans of beer from a blue cooler. When Tosha saw Gus she straightened up, beer in hand.

"Augusta," she said evenly. "I see you found a friend at the party already."

Gus dropped Jack's hand, then regretted it instantly. But it was too late to grab it again without looking ridiculous. Half a dozen vendors stood in a circle by Bernie's van, eyeing Gus but waiting for Tosha to do the talking. They looked at Jack as if he was the only dog invited to a cat's party.

"We're friends," Gus said, trying not to sound defensive.

"I can see that," Tosha replied.

"I mean you and me," Gus continued, feigning a light tone. "Why didn't you tell me you were setting up in this part of the parking lot? I would've moved my van over."

"It was a last-minute decision," Ricardo said.

Jack stepped closer to the group. "It's a big parking lot, but we're all here to celebrate the Fourth. We should join up and have one party like we usually do."

Silence hemmed in the group.

"No name tags, no worries," Jack said. "Midsummer Madness as usual." A note in his voice prompted Gus to step closer and take his hand again.

"Thought we'd do it a little different this year," Hank said.

Gus didn't like the expressions she saw in the semicircle. Without asking, they were forcing her to choose sides. Or were they? They hadn't invited her to join them or offered her a drink. Was the tight-knit group already shutting her out?

"Lease vendors are sticking together and having our own party this year," Ricardo said. "Sign of solidarity." He raised his beer can on the last words, making him look as if he was willing to lead a slightly unsteady revolution.

"I didn't know that," Gus said.

Tosha snapped the lid down on the cooler. "Like he said, it was a last-minute decision. You're free to do whatever you want."

Someone set off firecrackers nearby, piercing the silence between Gus and Jack and the lease vendors, whose numbers were growing as more chairs and coolers appeared by the hot-dog and fry vans.

"I should get over there before somebody sets something on fire," Jack said. Gus felt his grip on her hand tighten. He was offering her a graceful exit.

She couldn't take it.

"I'll be over in a few minutes," she told Jack. As he left the circle of headlights and tension, Gus faced the lease vendors. Her friends, she thought, who'd met at her shop, put her in charge of finding a solution to their contract woes, visited her when she was down, cheered her when she shot the boss in the back of the head with a rubber band…but they weren't applauding her now. This was a slap in the face.

For them.

She'd shown up hand in hand with Jack

Hamilton, the man who'd cheated them on their contracts, offered no explanation or apology and refused to even talk to them.

Oh, she'd talked to him plenty tonight. But it hadn't done any of the lease vendors or herself a single bit of good. She'd opened a ten-pound can of *what the heck was I thinking.*

Bernie barreled around the corner of his van. "I was just taking a leak over by the fence and I swear I saw Jack Hamilton talking to you guys. He wasn't giving you no trouble, was he?"

"Not all of us," Tosha said, looking directly at Gus.

"Good. Thought maybe he caught wind of last night's meeting."

Tosha wheeled on Bernie and gave him a look that said *shut up.*

"Last night's meeting?" Gus asked. "I didn't... Did we... But..." She gave up trying to phrase the question. She could read their faces. They'd had a meeting without her. They'd planned this party without her. She tried to keep her face under control. Her eyes smarted, her lip trembled. She wavered between explaining herself to the group and telling them all to mind their own business. But neither choice would do her any good.

"You've been really busy," Tosha said.

"We're all busy," Gus replied.

No one said anything.

"The weather's been great. The crowds huge. I thought we were all busy."

More silence.

"And that's a good thing," Gus continued. "We're all doing all right...aren't we?"

She hated the sound of her own voice. She seemed as if she was pleading her case, but her crime was...well, it was ridiculous. Her crime, in their eyes, was being too friendly with the boss. If they only knew—and they would by this time tomorrow—about her ride on the Star Spiral, they wouldn't even be talking to her.

"I'm not too busy to come to a vendor meeting," Gus said.

"You've been extra busy with the STRIPE thing for the past ten days," Tosha said. Her tone had softened, but the party was still on pause. "Those Hamiltons have had you jumping."

"I'm not jumping," Gus said.

"And there was the article in today's paper,"

Ricardo said. “All nice about the STRIPE and you helping with it.”

“I haven’t seen today’s paper yet.”

“Nice pictures of you.”

“The article was good for the park and for all of us. I didn’t mind doing it. It’s good PR.”

“I guess so,” Ricardo said.

“And there’s nothing wrong with a lease vendor running the STRIPE, is there? I’m sure you’ve all helped out over the years. Right?”

Tosha shook her head and no one said anything. Bernie opened the cooler and grabbed a few cans. Some of the younger summer employees stopped by when they saw the open cooler.

“Hey, Bernie. No fries tonight?” one of them asked.

“It’s a holiday.”

The guy who ran the Star Spiral, Ben, was in the group and grabbed a beer. Gus froze on sight of him, knowing he could blow her evening the rest of the way to pieces.

“What’s cookin’, baker lady?” He grinned at her. “Where’s your date?”

She stared at him, willing him to fill his mouth with beer and walk away. Not that it would matter. She realized now that people were already talking about her being too cozy with the Hamiltons. As if that was a crime.

Looking around the group, she understood that, in their eyes, she'd committed a serious offense. The summer workers started to walk away. Gus took one last look around the circle, hoping for some sympathy, but she wasn't going to win this battle tonight. She had to leave before she embarrassed herself or said something she'd regret.

She turned and walked across the dark lot, thinking for a full five seconds the lease vendors might call her back or invite her to stay. They didn't.

Gus stood in darkness and solitude, loud parties to the left and right. She looked up and there it was. The midnight-blue sky behind the racing white lights of the coasters. The picture she carried from that long, exhilarating day when she was a child. She wished her father could pick her up and carry her home tonight. But he was on the other side of the world and she was grown up now.

She sat on the pavement, still warm from soaking up the day's midsummer heat. Chin on knees, she watched the Ferris wheel's lights trace a circle of color and start again. In front of it, the Silver Streak's crisp white lights chased the length of track and back again. Then it was all gone, blotted out by a tall, dark figure.

"You're blocking my view, Jack."

He sat next to her, their sides barely brushing. "This is my favorite perspective of the park," he said. "When I was little, I'd always stop and look back as my mother hauled me to our house on the Old Road after a long day. I'd make her pause and look just for a second. I tried to take a picture of it when I got my first camera, but since the flash went about ten feet, of course it didn't work."

"You could try it again. Cameras have come a long way."

"I don't think so. Some things just exist in…just can't be captured."

"Tell you a secret, Jack. This is my favorite view of Starlight Point, too."

"I know. I heard you say that at the STRIPE training. Childhood memory for you, too?"

She nodded. "Long, fun day with my parents and my aunt. My dad carried me to the car, but I'll never forget looking back over his shoulder all the way out. I tried to stamp it on my memory so I could keep it forever." She laughed. "And here I am. I guess I didn't have to do that. It's still here. I started to think I belonged here, like this was my home. But the people I work with don't seem to think so."

Jack put his hand on her knee. "It all looks so perfect from here. You don't see the sweat, smell the stale food, hear the family disputes about where the beach entrance is or what time they should all meet up. All the magic, none of the problems."

"Too good to be true."

"I want to see you again tomorrow."

"You probably will. You know where I work. Which reminds me, I should go. It'll be an early morning at the bakery." She got to her feet.

"That's not what I meant."

"I know. But we're on opposing teams."

"We don't have to be," he said.

"Then fix it. You caused this mess, you can fix it."

"No," he said decisively.

"No, you can't fix it?" Anger replaced bittersweet frustration in her voice.

"No," he said, "I didn't cause it."

Gus crossed her arms and stepped back. "Isn't your name on those contracts?"

"Yes."

"So?" she asked.

He turned and looked at Starlight Point. Thousands of people were streaming through its gates, people who'd soon be in a temper-flaring traffic jam. "You make a lot of assumptions," he finally said. "So has everyone else. You have no idea what—"

"Does this have anything to do with Consolidated Theme Parks?" she asked.

"No," he roared, drawing attention from all over the parking lot.

She felt as if she'd drilled a hole in the side of an overburdened dam. "Then tell me," she said, her voice softer. "You can't claim there's some big mystery explaining why it's not your fault and then refuse to talk."

"I own this place." His words were cold. "I can do anything I want."

More amateur fireworks and noisemakers cut the night followed by a chorus of horn honking.

"The hell with it," he said. "I'm going home. If they burn the place down, it saves me a lot of trouble."

Gus stared at him. "I don't understand you."

When he didn't answer, she pulled her keys from her pocket and turned toward her van.

"You're not staying for the party?" he asked.

She sighed and considered her answer. "Which party? Which party should I go to, Jack?"

He didn't reply, just stood, hands in pockets, staring at his amusement park.

"That's the whole problem," she said, stepping back and heading for her van.

CHAPTER TWENTY

"GOT ANYTHING YOU need me to hit with a big hammer?" Jack asked.

Mel shut the toolbox on the side of his truck and leaned against the driver's door. "Maybe," he said, "but you'd have to fire yourself for damaging your own property."

"Doesn't sound so bad. Being in charge of this circus is a pain in the neck anyway."

Pulling out his cell phone, Mel glanced at it and slipped it back in the pocket of his navy blue work uniform. "I'm on my way to the Octopus ride in Kiddieland. Sprung a big oily leak a few minutes ago. But I've got five minutes to listen while you tell me why you've got a firecracker up your rear today. I'm guessing your Fourth of July wasn't quite as good as rumor would have me believe."

Jack palmed a bead of sweat off his forehead. Mel had managed to park his truck in the one area of direct sun in the maintenance garage's lot.

"Can't do anything around here without people talking."

"You took an extralong ride on the Star Spiral with the woman who's had your tongue hanging out all summer—you're right. Don't see why anyone would care about that."

Jack grabbed a bottle of water from the cooler in the bed of Mel's truck. "You're really helpful."

"Just confirming the gossip. I'd only heard it five times in the past two days, and you know I'm too delicate to bring it up directly. Hope it was good, by the way."

Jack shook his head. "I don't know."

"What's the problem?"

"You haven't heard that part? She won't talk to me now. Totally avoiding me."

"Maybe she didn't like the ride," Mel said.

"Nothing wrong with the Spiral."

"Well, if that isn't it, why do you think she doesn't want to see your sorry self?"

"Could be mad at me," Jack said.

"I think she was already. Aren't all the vendors ready to march on your office? I heard

Dorothea was fending them off with a stapler."

"Nothing has changed with the vendors."

"Maybe there's your problem," Mel said. "Gus thought going for a ride with you would change things for the better. And it didn't."

Jack stared down his friend. He threw the half-empty water bottle thirty feet across the parking lot, hitting the Dumpster with a vicious clang.

"I could be wrong," Mel observed coolly.

"Darn right you are."

Mel's cell phone chirped, but he ignored it. "I'd love to help you, but figuring out why women are mad is like mapping the ocean floor. I'd be in over my head. Maybe you should ask her."

"Tried. When I stopped to see her yesterday and today, her employees said she was too busy."

"Send flowers?"

"They'll be delivered tomorrow. I was too late with my order today."

"You could ask your sister. Evie's tight with Gus. She's got her feet in both camps but still manages to get people to like her. You should try that."

"I asked Evie. She won't help me. Either she doesn't know or she's not talking."

"Women," Mel said. "Wish you luck, boss. I'm off to wrangle a sick octopus, and that's a piece of cake compared to your problems."

SEVERAL DAYS LATER, Gus put on dark sunglasses for her walk from the Last Chance to the Midway Bakery.

She couldn't take back her feelings for Jack—didn't want to—and didn't feel like apologizing for it. She also didn't feel like talking about it, especially to Jack.

He'd stopped by her bakery every day, but she'd managed to be busy. Sending summer employees to the front to dismiss the boss was probably a violation of workplace etiquette, but Gus figured she'd already broken all the usual rules by kissing the big kahuna.

Early in the morning two days ago, she'd heard his bicycle bell ring over and over outside her midway bakery, but she'd refused to roll up the front awning, deliberately sending doughnuts into the fryer instead. Sizzling covered up ringing if you threw in enough grease.

Evie had given her about seventy-five easy

segues into a how-about-your-feelings-for-my-brother conversation, but each time Gus put on an obtuse expression and pretended to be consumed by icing cookies.

When flowers arrived, Evie smelled them and exclaimed over their beauty, waiting while Gus read the card. "It's a thank-you," Gus said. "For being the STRIPE sergeant."

Total lie. It really said, "I would give anything just to talk to you."

Jack had signed the card himself. And it was tempting—so tempting—to talk to him. But she didn't trust herself. She'd already served him a batch of her feelings and she couldn't give away much more without risking the whole thing.

And so she hoped—unreasonably—to avoid him until Labor Day.

"Augusta."

So much for that plan.

He stood framed in the back entrance of her Last Chance bakery, dark suit, white shirt, hungry look in his eyes. Her heart thudded in her ears. It had been almost five days since their ride on the Star Spiral. And she could still feel every whisper of his lips on hers.

Gus glanced at the counter Jack had placed

her on the night of the robbery. She shivered, thinking about it. He'd been her hero that night. Could still be. Maybe.

Loud gunfire erupted outside, pierced by a train whistle, and Jack jumped through the door. "Never get used to that, I swear."

"I was just leaving," Gus said, wanting and *not* wanting to be alone with him.

"I can walk with you," Jack offered, approaching her slowly as if he thought she might run away.

"I was thinking of taking the train."

"No, you weren't. I don't think you've had time for any rides this summer."

"Just one," she said. There was no need to remind him which one.

"Walk with me. Please."

She stared at him, tempted to say no. But she couldn't spend the rest of the season avoiding him. Especially now that she'd seen him again. Up close, he exuded the same magnetic force that had been getting her in trouble all summer.

"Be prepared to keep up with me, because I've got plenty to do before I hit the ferry for downtown," she said, trying to sound crisp and efficient.

They left the bakery, passed the theater and crossed the bridge onto the trail before Jack spoke.

"You've been avoiding me," he said.

"Maybe you've been avoiding me." Considering the difficult position she was in because of him, Gus felt justified being a pain in the neck.

"Give me a break," he said.

Gus said nothing, walking at a punishing pace. Every vendor they passed saw them. The dark sunglasses did nothing to disguise her, and Jack was exceptionally obvious with his height and trademark suit. Starlight Point guests gave Jack a second look as he passed them. She knew what they assumed. He owned the place. Had to. A tall, handsome man dressed for business at an amusement park? Who else could he be? Gus risked a glance at him. This was the only thing he could be. Jack belonged to Starlight Point as much as it belonged to him.

"I have the impression you're being forced to choose sides," he finally said.

"I try hard to avoid being forced into anything," she replied. "But it doesn't always pan out."

"Point taken."

The gates for the train crossing swung down, making them stop at the head of the trail and wait with the other guests. The train slowly chugged forward. Jack took Gus's hand and tugged her under a nearby shade tree in a relatively secluded spot behind a guessing game.

"I don't regret what happened between us on the Star Spiral, and I'm not going to pretend I don't want it to happen again."

"Too many people around right now."

"You know what I mean," Jack snapped.

"I do. And I'm *not* going to say that I *disagree*," she said, mimicking his tone.

"So?"

What did he want her to say? Being with him was like giving in and eating a whole pie. Sweet. Satisfying. Wonderful.

But they were on opposite sides of a fight. He was forbidden fruit. Though the other vendors had already rejected her, so maybe she had nothing to lose. Except her sense of responsibility to people who had begun to treat her like family. Until she'd betrayed them.

"So," she said, "open the contracts and remove the clause that's alienating me and all the other vendors, and we'll talk."

"You can't use those contracts to drive a wedge between us."

Gus took a deep breath and let it out, focusing on the smoke billowing from the passing train. "Everyone else is," she said quietly.

Jack crossed his arms over his chest. "Do you think I don't know what it's like to be torn between two things—both of them valuable, one of them…"

"One of them what?"

He sat on a steel bench by the fence where they stood. "One of them so important you couldn't give it up even if you wanted to."

Gus pulled off her sunglasses and stood directly in front of Jack. "I don't want to choose sides. I wish I could be on everyone's side."

"That's not possible sometimes."

"I'm a Sagittarius. We always think it's possible."

The train cleared the tracks and people rushed by their bench, probably never noticing them. Gus stood still, watching Jack's face.

"I should go," she said. "It's a busy day and I left a small crew up front. They're probably elbow deep in dough and wondering where I am."

"I think I'll sit here awhile, watch the crowds."

"It's your park—do what you want."

"I wish I could."

She turned to walk away and he grabbed her hand. "Augusta, it feels like there's an ocean between us right now, but I believe you'd be there with a life ring if I needed it."

"You're a good swimmer, Jack," she said, pulling her hand gently from his and walking away.

CHAPTER TWENTY-ONE

"I'M TOAST," HANK SAID, handing Gus a hot dog. It had been a quiet weekday at the Point. Most guests had already eaten and were lining up for their last rides. Gus had enough cookies in the case for the evening rush as people stocked up for the car ride home. And she was tired, ready to call it a night.

"My bookkeeping is a nightmare and I'm never gonna get my June reports done by the July fifteenth deadline," Hank continued.

"Sorry to hear that," Gus said. She reminded herself to thank Evie, who had completed the monthly statement practically before the month was over. Gus didn't *love* handing over twenty percent of her profits to Starlight Point. But, she reasoned, Starlight Point was the reason she *had* those profits. The revenue from her stands at the Point was bolstering her downtown shop and getting her closer to her dream of making Aunt Augusta's Bakery a success.

Hank smiled at Gus, his eyes wide. "You know anything about the computer program that does those spreadsheets?"

"Just enough to get by. I've handed it all over to my summer accountant."

"Who you got?"

"Evie Hamilton."

"Oh. Thought she just worked for you."

"Nope. Manages my hotel bakeshop and does the books for all three shops here at the Point."

Hank handed Gus the ketchup bottle. "Not worried about sleeping with the enemy?"

Gus winced. "Evie isn't anybody's enemy."

"I don't know," Hank said. "Not sure I like the idea of a Hamilton sticking their nose in my business."

"Starlight Point is their business, the bakery is mine. I'm trying to keep my feet on the right side of the line," Gus said.

Ricardo and Tosha walked over. Gus wondered if they'd been watching from their stands across the midway. When it came to confidential information, Hank was definitely the weakest link. His secret sauce recipe was no secret, and it was just as well, because he would crack under pressure faster than a microwaved hot dog.

"You don't want people nosing around your business, Hank," Ricardo said. He looked pointedly at Gus. "Especially when you're not a hundred percent sure what side they're on."

"We told you last night we'd help you with your computer spreadsheet," Tosha added.

"Almost forgot that," Hank said. "I was in a hurry to get out of there after the meeting because I forgot to set my DVR for my favorite show. *Best Places for a Hot Dog in North America.* Hoping they'll take the suggestions I sent in after last season."

"Another meeting?" Gus asked.

Tosha rolled her eyes. "I didn't think you'd be interested," she said.

"I thought we were going to make plans together—if not for this year's contracts, then for next year."

Ricardo shoved his hands in his pockets. "You said yourself that Jack Hamilton doesn't have to dirty his hands by talking to us. We signed the contract and we have to live with it."

"That's not exactly what I said."

"General idea."

"So, if that's not what you talked about at the meetings I've missed, what did you discuss?"

"Things," Tosha said.

"Like what?"

"Like the same things we've been talking about for ten, fifteen, twenty years. You're new this summer, so I guess you wouldn't have some of the same interests as those of us who've been here practically our whole lives."

Gus felt as if she'd been kicked in the back of the knees. She was speechless.

"And since you're so cozy with the Hamiltons, maybe you can tell us why an appraiser's been hanging around, measuring up our shops," Tosha said.

"An appraiser?"

Tosha and Ricardo nodded. "Been making his way down our side of the midway all day. Doing inspections, taking notes, asking questions."

Gus looked at her uneaten hot dog on Hank's counter. Her appetite was gone, replaced by a Titanic-sized sinking in her gut.

"Maybe," she said, "he's from the insurance company?"

"Asked him that," Ricardo said. "He said no then clammed up."

"So what could be the reason?" Hank asked. "Hamilton owns all our shops already. We just lease 'em. Why'd a guy appraise his own property?"

"Could be he wants to see how valuable it is so he can offer our spots to someone else next summer. We only have a one-season lease, and I think we're getting an idea of just how important we are to the new owners," Tosha grumbled.

"Wait a minute," Gus said. "Is it just the vendor shops being appraised? No other parts of the property?"

"Far as we know," Tosha said, "but we don't exactly have our fingers in the rest of the business." She crossed her arms over her chest, covering up the cheerful ice-cream cone on her pink apron. "If Jack Hamilton thinks we can be easily replaced, he's got another think coming. He's about to find out just how valuable we all are."

She and Ricardo stalked off toward the long line of lease-vendor stands on the other side of the midway.

"Don't know what to think," Hank said. He

picked up Gus's hot dog and took a big bite. "Trouble always makes me hungry."

A group of teenagers lined up at the counter, breaking up the conversation and providing an escape for Gus. She was done for the day.

She headed straight for the park gate that led to the marina. The eight o'clock ferry would leave in ten minutes. Plenty of time for her to hand over a buck fifty and find her favorite spot. On the starboard side, there was a single seat carved out between the door and a cabinet for life-jacket storage. Since most people enjoyed a day at the park with friends or family, she usually had no competition for the single-rider slot.

Until tonight. When she stepped onto the boat, the first thing she saw was a man sitting in her seat. Mel Preston.

She paused in front of him. The mood she was in, it was tempting to plant her foot under him and shove him out of her seat.

He glanced up, his eyes widening in the quickly fading daylight. He grinned, and Gus felt some of her tension slide off her shoulders.

"Must be my lucky day," he said. "Didn't think so this morning when I had to take the ferry to work like a teenager with no car privileges."

Gus sat on the bench across from Mel. "I take the ferry every now and then. And I'm no teenager."

"What about your pink van?"

"It's a gas hog. The ferry's a lot cheaper."

The boat horn sounded twice and the captain backed the half-empty ferry out of the slip. It was a beautiful July evening, with most employees staying until closing, even after their shifts had ended, and most guests choosing to do the same.

"My son likes to stop in your downtown bakery and get a treat—if it's still open when we get home from the Point," Mel said. "He likes the apple fritters."

Gus glanced across the water at Bayside as the ferry swung around. "I haven't spent much time in my downtown shop this summer." She looked back at Mel, who smiled sympathetically and nodded. "I have a habit of taking on more than I can handle."

"One of the things that makes you interesting," he said. "And you have help downtown, right? Your aunt—the real Aunt Augusta—runs it."

She nodded.

"Thought so. I read the article about you in the paper. Gonna have to get your approval on a cake in a couple weeks. My son turns five July twenty-ninth."

"I'm sure it'll be wonderful."

"Hope so. You know, I thought this year's STRIPE topic might be the worst one yet, but then I got to thinking. Since my ex drops into town a couple times a year when she's feeling guilty, I'm pretty much the only parent my son's got. Guess it's not a bad thing to know how to make him a birthday cake."

"What's your son's name?"

"Ross."

"It must be fun to have a little boy."

"It is. His mother happens to be in town this week. Which is why I'm taking the ferry. Her car died, and I left her with my truck so she could take Ross to the park. Guess I'll have to fix her car if I want to get rid of her and get my truck back."

Gus said nothing, watching the sunset on the bay and replaying the scene at Hank's stand over and over in her mind.

"Sorry I'm boring you with my family saga," Mel said after a few minutes of silence.

Gus laughed. "I'm not bored. It's nice to have someone to talk to on the ferry. Where does your wife—"

"Ex-wife."

"Ex-wife," Gus said, "go when she leaves?"

"Anywhere that's not here. She's not from Bayside, doesn't see what's so great about Starlight Point… I guess she likes the city, seeing new faces. I'm content to see the old faces and the friends I've had forever."

"I've moved around a lot, but Bayside has always been home base for me."

"And you're here to stay?"

"I hope so. I'm tired of following my parents wherever Dad's job takes them. I have to settle down and build a life for myself, and I don't have any other family aside from my aunt. Living here, I've got a loft above my bakery and a great view."

"And Starlight Point?"

"That's part of the view."

"I mean, is that why you want to stick around?"

Gus's glance strayed from Mel and lingered on the retreating lights of the Point. Could she see herself working at Starlight Point next summer and the summers that followed, seasons stretching before her like waves? Running her bakeries and coming up with new cookies and treats? Was it even an option? She turned back to Mel.

"Do you have any idea why an appraiser might be nosing around the vendor shops on the midway?"

"Not just the vendors," he said. Then he shut up.

"Why is Starlight Point being appraised?"

Mel pulled a tape measure off his tool belt and played with it, pulling the tape out a few inches and letting it snap back. Over and over. He didn't look up. Gus wanted to reach over, grab the tape measure and throw it overboard.

"Fine," she said. "You know something, but you're not going to tell me. I know you're a loyal friend."

"You're Jack's friend, too. More than a friend."

"Is that what Jack thinks?"

"Don't you know what he thinks?"

She sighed, not answering. She wondered how much Jack confided in Mel. Didn't matter. Mel seemed like the kind of guy who wouldn't hand over info in exchange for a bribe.

"I'd kill for beer and pizza right now," Mel commented. "Or one of your cookies."

Then again, maybe he *could* be bought. But that was cheap, beneath her, even in desperate times.

The horn sounded and the ferry bumped the Bayside dock a second later. The other passengers lined up at the low, swinging door, waiting for the captain to clear them to get off. The line of people between Gus and Mel ended their deadlocked conversation, and neither of them renewed it as they walked up the dock.

"Need a ride?" Gus offered. "The van is parked one block up."

"Nope. Believe it or not, the ex is waiting for me in my truck. Wonders never cease."

"People surprise me all the time," Gus said. "Good night, Mel."

"One thing… You've got more influence with the other vendors than you think. Might come a time when you have to put your friendship to good use."

"For which side?"

"Everybody's."

CHAPTER TWENTY-TWO

"How much do you think the repair will cost?" Jack asked, hoping the maintenance man had good news for once.

"Couple thousand for the new lines, fuel meters on top of that. Should probably get a new pump while we're at it."

Jack sat on the edge of the marina dock and let his feet dangle. His dress shoes almost reached the water. "Too much for this year. If we just cap the gas line that runs to this set of docks, boats could still fuel up on the other dock. Right?"

"Guess so."

"And we could save this job for next summer," Jack said.

"Fine by me. Summer's half over as it is."

"Save what for next year?" Evie asked.

"Fixing the fuel lines for Dock A. This marina's getting old," Jack said. "Hate to do it, but..." He shrugged.

"It won't kill boaters to pull up to the other dock," Evie said. She leaned closer to Jack and lowered her voice. "We don't need one more expense this year."

"That's what I thought, too."

"I'm picking up Mom and getting some dinner. Want to come?"

"Nope. It's a nice evening. I might knock off early and take the kayak out since the boss isn't around."

Evie ruffled his hair as he swung his feet back and forth. "I love you, Jack. You're my favorite brother."

She started to walk away but then her footsteps on the decking stopped. "Hey, Gus. Heading home?"

"Catching the ferry."

"I'm going out for a quick dinner then I'll be back to close the shops for the night."

"Thanks. I have some flowers to make for an upcoming wedding cake. Fancy gum-paste lilies that'll take me all night. Unless my aunt got them done already."

"Hope so, for your sake," Evie said, her voice trailing off as she walked away.

Jack stood and stepped in front of Augusta as she made her way down the dock.

Gus blew out a breath. "I have to get in line for the boat."

"I should warn you about the ferry," he said quietly, his lips close to her ear.

She stepped away, out of the circle of temptation.

"Oh?" she asked.

"Heard you rode with Mel Preston a few nights ago," he said, grinning. "I advise you to steer clear of him."

"I thought he was your best friend."

"He is. But when it comes to women, he's always after the unattainable."

"Really?"

Jack nodded. "Long history. Seems to choose the ones who want to get away, but he likes it right here."

"That's what he said."

Jack's phone rang. He ignored it.

"For a long time, I thought he was in love with my sister June," Jack continued.

"The one who's not here," Gus said.

"See what I mean?"

"Could be a coincidence."

"She's coming into town tomorrow for a few days, but she'll be in a big hurry to get back to New York. Hope she doesn't break his heart while she's here."

Gus wanted to ask why June was coming. Tomorrow was July 18, one day before the day Evie had mysteriously asked for off. This time, it wasn't her mother's birthday or her brother's birthday, and she'd been completely closemouthed about her plans. It didn't take a lot of imagination to know that some serious family business was happening on July 19. How could she ask Jack to fill in the details?

His phone rang again.

"You should answer that," Gus said. "I have to go or I'll miss the ferry."

THE LAST THING Jack wanted to do was answer his phone, but he hoped to get rid of whoever it was and catch up with Gus. They had too much unfinished and unsaid between them.

Distracted by the evening light on Gus's hair, Jack needed a moment to understand what his chief of security was saying. The incoming ferry—which mercifully had only ten people on it—had engine trouble and was being towed back to Bayside that very moment.

Not a disaster, but if Gus didn't get on the

one leaving in about thirty seconds, she was in for a long wait.

Jack hit the dock speed walking, just in time to watch the ferry pull away.

Without Augusta.

He was sorry about her bad luck, but he thought fate might be on his side for the first time this summer. He spoke briefly with a teenage ferry hostess on the dock, suggesting what she might tell the guests, who would be curious about the long wait ahead.

Jack lined up next to Augusta. “Missed your boat,” he said.

“I was distracted.”

“Sorry about that.”

“No, you’re not.”

“If it gives me an excuse for waiting with you, then I’m not.”

“You don’t need to wait for the ferry,” Gus said. “You live here.”

She tapped her foot on the marina decking and breathed out through her nose. Her long brown hair moved with the lake breeze as she eyed the ferry line.

“You’re beautiful,” Jack said.

She rolled her eyes.

“Even when you do that.”

She almost smiled.

"I can help you," he said.

Now she raised her eyebrows and looked straight at him. "So you're offering me a ride home?"

"Not exactly. I thought I'd be charming company while you waited."

She tossed her purse on a bench and sat down.

"So generous."

Jack grinned, sliding onto the bench next to her.

"I know. I'm a busy guy and here I am sitting by the water with you."

She snorted. "So you can't command the waves and get me a ride home on the back of a mermaid or anything? Maybe you don't have the power you think you do."

He laughed. "I don't have any magic. But—"

His eyes fell on the thirty-foot motorboat his father kept in perfect running shape. Jack hadn't thought about it since his father's death. Ford Hamilton must have put it in the water before he died because there it was, bobbing placidly at the end of its ropes right along the dock. The *Starlight*. Where it always was. As if it was waiting for Ford to come back. Or for Jack to need it.

He'd used it plenty of times, usually with his family. Day trips to the offshore islands, water-skiing and tubing when he felt adventurous. Never as often as they wanted because summers were fast and busy.

"But what?" Gus asked, apparently tired of waiting for him to go on.

"I have a boat."

"Of course you do," she said, giving him another eye roll. "You can probably afford a second by the end of the year with all the cookies I'm selling. Maybe you could name it after me."

"I could take you home."

She looked at him pointedly. "You could take me home in your car."

"Sure. But my car is clear across the parking lot at my house. And this is more fun."

"I can wait. Next ferry is only twenty-five minutes away."

"Actually, it's not. That phone call was about the other ferry. Engine trouble. Looks like you'll be waiting almost an hour."

She turned her attention to the calm bay, the sunset and the line of people already waiting for the next ferry. Lots of people. Chatty summer workers. Crying children.

"What kind of boat do you have?"

Jack grinned. Pointed. "That one."

He waited for her reaction, having no idea what she expected. But it was the kind of boat that impressed even people who didn't care about boats. Gleaming white fiberglass, shining navy blue hull. His father loved boats, and the marina staff considered it their personal mission to keep the *Starlight* pristine.

Gus eyed the boat, clearly considering his offer.

A little boy waiting with his family for the next ferry leaned over and threw up hot dogs and popcorn off the dock. It made a horrific splash when it hit the water.

Jack's grin widened.

"How about a ride now?"

"I'll take it."

It took only a minute to get the keys from the dockmaster, who told him the boat was fueled up and ready. Just in case.

"Appreciate it," he said.

The trip to downtown Bayside was short. With the powerful engine, the boat could probably zip across to the city docks in ten minutes. He could have Augusta in her lake-view loft before the next ferry even tied up at the dock.

"Make yourself comfortable," he said over the quiet engine. Gus sat on the wide seat across the back of the boat, watching as several dockhands helped Jack unhook and cast off. In no time, he'd cleared the marina break wall. Jack turned on the navigation lights and took his time, heading for the center of the bay.

"I have a question," he said. "But I'm almost afraid to ask it."

"Go ahead."

"I don't want to put you in a weird position or make you feel like you're betraying anyone's confidence."

"I'm already in the middle of things between Starlight Point—you—and the vendors, if that's what you're talking about."

"I know. And it is." Jack steered standing up by the captain's chair. "My question is, what's the mood of the vendors? What are they thinking long-term?"

Gus tilted her head to the side. "You seem nervous, Jack."

"Should I be?"

"As you know, we already had the meeting where we flung insults at you. Then we burned a straw creation that looked very much like Jack Hamilton at the next one." She smiled. "Plotted your overthrow at another meeting, and then just settled in for a get-drunk-and-complain session at the next one."

"I probably had it coming."

"You think?"

"So, if I may ask, what's next with the vendors?"

"You mean this season or next?"

"Both, I guess."

"They're nervous," she said, crossing one long leg over the other. "They don't know what will happen next year."

"Not sure what you mean."

"There are rumors," Gus said. "Appraisers have been in their shops. They've been in my shops. Not a whole lot of reasons we can think of why our stores would be assessed."

"What do they think the appraisals are for?"

"Come on, Jack. People aren't stupid. You raised the vendors' rates, you're having their stores appraised. What do you think they think?"

Jack knew he was playing with fire, but he had her full attention. No walking away, no prying ears. He had to know.

"Tell me what they've heard. Why they think this is happening," he prodded.

Gus sighed. "Are you kidding me? Fine. I'll tell you exactly what they think and I'm not betraying them because it's what anyone would think in their positions. They think you no longer feel any loyalty to them. They think you plan to run them out with higher rates. They think you want to replace them with cheaper vendors or take over their stores yourself so you can keep all the profits."

Dull heavy pressure weighted Jack's chest. Hearing the list of his supposed crimes was like listening to a judge pronouncing a sentence.

"But I don't," he said, sounding more defensive than he intended. "I can't tell you tonight why the appraisals are going on, but I will say they're happening all over Starlight Point, not just the vendors."

"Okay." She didn't look convinced.

"I'm sorry the vendors have the wrong idea about my plans. I would've thought they'd have more trust in me."

Gus frowned and raised both eyebrows.

"I know. They're mad about the contracts."

"Can you blame them? Me?"

"No, but I have my reasons."

"Maybe you should come out and tell them your reasons. Tell *me* your reasons. Try a little openness. You might be surprised how people would respond to some honest communication from you."

"My business is my business. Mine and my family's," he said coldly. He was tired of defending an indefensible position.

"You think it's just your business?" Gus asked. "Not to Tosha and Bernie and Hank and Ricardo and everyone else. And me. Your business—Starlight Point—is also their business. It's been their livelihood and their summer home for years. They've helped make Starlight Point what it is. Unless you show that you value them, I'm afraid you're going to be really sorry."

"What is that supposed to mean?" A flicker of fear raced through him at her threat.

"Figure it out."

Jack turned and looked at Starlight Point, its coaster lights and familiar skyline reassuring. He was out of options, time to sink or swim.

His eyes fell on Augusta—legs crossed, purse on lap, avoiding eye contact.

He cut the engine. Threw out the anchor. That got her attention.

"Kidnapping me?" she asked.

"We'd still be moving if I were kidnapping you."

"So what are you doing?" She didn't look afraid or even especially mad. Exasperated maybe.

"I need to talk to you," he said, trying for a neutral tone.

He sat next to her, but made sure he wasn't touching her. Jack took a calming breath. And another. His heart was racing. Aside from his mother and sisters, Augusta was the first person he was going to tell. Not even Mel, although Jack knew he suspected.

"I'm listening," Gus said. Her expression softened a little. Maybe it was just the peachy sunset lighting, but it was enough.

"I always knew I would run the Point someday," he said.

She nodded, a tiny smile curving her lips.

"And I thought I knew how."

"You do know how. I mean, you are. Right?" she said.

"Ever since I could walk—and in Betty's wagon before that—I went to work with Dad each day in the summer. All day. He took me everywhere. Showed me everything. Included me in decisions. Made me feel like I knew exactly how Starlight Point was run. In recent years, I thought I was his partner. Thought I was running it. At least my half."

The sudden, ragged pain in Jack's chest stopped him. His eyes burned. He got up abruptly and walked across the deck, rocking the boat with his movement.

"I thought I knew everything, Gus." His voice shook even though he fought it.

He sensed her right behind him. Felt a hand on his shoulder.

"Until two months ago. When Dad didn't wake up one morning."

Jack hadn't shed a tear since the funeral, instead throwing himself into running the Point and trying to outpace his problems. He leaned down, hands gripping the railing along the side of the boat. Grief for his father choked him. Blinded him. Tears raced over his cheeks.

He would not let her see him cry. Would not turn around.

He thought of the hours he'd spent with his dad. After working here every summer during college, coming home afterward and working year-round. Talking, planning. Practically sharing an office. The obvious heir apparent. His chest was so tight he couldn't breathe.

How could he not have known his father's secret?

Arms slid around him from behind, holding him in a silent embrace. He forced his attention to the present. The water. The fading sun. The red navigation lights along the side of the boat. Anything solid he could focus on.

Jack pulled himself together with a great shuddering effort. And he didn't know if he could have done it without the strong, sweet arms around his waist, the scent of vanilla and buttercream that always wafted from Augusta's hair.

He turned and pulled her against him, cradling her head against his chest, not letting her see his face. Not yet.

She seemed to understand. Not prying, just holding him on the gently rocking boat.

"I thought I knew everything," he repeated. "But I didn't."

Gus was silent, listening.

"When you die," Jack said, "you're at the mercy of the living. I guess you take some secrets to your grave, but everything else is right there for everyone to see."

Jack stroked Gus's back methodically, drawing calmness and resolve from her. "After my father's funeral, the next day, I went to his office. Our office. My office now. I opened the account books for the Point."

"You'd seen them before, right?" Gus asked quietly. It was the first time she'd spoken.

Jack shook his head. "No. My dad kept tight control. He gave me a budget, expected me to stay in it. I thought he was teaching me a lesson on fiscal responsibility. I thought he stayed in his budget, too."

His heart was going to explode. Anger. Shame. Grief. All the things he'd bottled up and avoided were squeezing his lungs, taking his breath.

Gus massaged his chest with her hands, making slow circles, repeating the motion in a soothing pattern. He tried to unclench every muscle in his body, tried to yield to her soft touch. But he wasn't done.

"Ford Hamilton had a lot to hide. He'd been

taking out loan upon loan for years. And none of us knew. Sure, we guessed he borrowed big for the new rides like that monstrosity the Sea Devil."

More soft circles massaged the pain out of the center of his chest, taking it to the outside. Gus looked up, met his eyes.

"I think I can guess the rest," she said.

"It's terrible. Massive loan for the Sea Devil. Small loans from different banks, loans taken out to pay off other loans. Most of them short-term, like he thought the money would be just around the corner."

Gus sighed. "He was an optimist."

"Irresponsible," Jack said with a quick shake of his head. "Unrealistic. Worst of all, secretive. Mom didn't even know."

"Does it hurt you that he never told you?"

Jack tilted his head back, looking at the darkening sky. "It kills me."

He buried his fingers in Augusta's soft hair, trying to rein in his emotions. He bit his lip. Hard. "It killed him," he finally said.

Gus reached up, smoothing his forehead, holding his face in both hands. There were tears in her eyes. "You don't have to say anything more. I understand what you've been doing. And why. But what happens next?"

"We hope to hang on to it."

"Is Consolidated Amusement Parks really trying to buy you out?"

"Not anymore. Evie and I got one of the banks to buy out most of the other loans so they're all in one place. We fought off Consolidated with that move a few weeks ago when June was home."

"I'm glad your sisters know about this. They're one-third owners, right?"

Jack nodded. "Mom knows, too. We're all in this together. That's why June's coming tomorrow. Bankers want a personal tour. Want to see we're different from Dad. Expect to see plans, a clean business model, a future where we can pay our debts. Even if it takes years."

"Or?"

"Or it's over."

Gus rubbed his neck and shoulders. Jack felt tension leaving his body under her strong fingers. Telling his mother and sisters had taken some of the pressure off, but they were in trouble right alongside him. Gus was different. She was a friend. More than a friend. And she had the most amazing hands.

"You're good at that," he murmured, letting her lull him into relaxation. Maybe he should sit down.

"I have freakishly strong hands," she said quietly. "From squeezing pastry bags. But this is more fun."

"Keep it up and I *will* kidnap you. I think we can get to Canada from here."

"Perfect," she said, smiling. "You can escape your debts and have a personal masseuse."

"I could never leave Starlight Point," he said, closing his eyes and letting his head fall forward.

"I know. You won't have to. You'll impress the bankers and use all the dough you're making off vendors like me to pay your loans. See? Happily-ever-after."

Jack opened one eye, almost afraid to see if she was serious.

"Kidding," she said. "About some of that. I know you'll impress the bankers because any transparency and planning is better than what your dad did. And they kept loaning *him* money. Right?"

Jack almost laughed. "Sad but true."

He could breathe again. The night air was

fresh but getting cooler. The lights on the boat stood out against the dark water.

"I should take you home like I promised. You held up your end of the bargain by listening. Now it's my turn."

CHAPTER TWENTY-THREE

GUS DROVE HER pink van to the Point early on Friday, July 19. She hadn't slept all night, so she'd stopped casting evil glances at her clock, gotten up and drunk coffee while the sun came up. Fridays were usually nuts. Her cookie supplies were down, there wasn't a single cupcake in the case, and she felt like it would be a huge doughnut day. If someone got there early enough to make dozens of them.

She hadn't seen Jack since the night before last, when he'd finally dropped her off at the downtown dock. He'd left a message on her voice mail to say he was thinking of her, but she knew he was preoccupied. Understandably. No doubt he was busy with his sisters and the new accountants they'd hired, doing everything they could to prepare for the bankers' visit.

She'd left a message on the machine in her shop, knowing her aunt would check it when she got in about eight. "Taking the van and going to the Point early. I'll bring it back this afternoon in case you need me to deliver anything. Have a great day! Love you, Gus."

The lone security guard waved her through, recognizing her pink van. She pulled into the Star Spiral lot. Not a single vehicle was there. It was early, but a few of the other vendors would usually have arrived by now. The dashboard clock said 6:07 a.m. when she switched off the van and climbed out.

Keys jingled in her hand, mocking the silent carousel, as she opened the side door of her midway bakery.

"Plenty of time to make dozens of doughnuts before the first crowds," she said to herself. She left the side door open, letting in the cool morning air and slanted sunshine. She dropped doughnuts into the fryer over and over, noticing that no one passed by the open door. Sizzling doughnuts and oven timers made early-morning music in her bakery, but not a sound came from the other vendor shops.

The carousel lurched into action, its music floating eerily over the silence. One hour until opening. She rolled up the front window shade and saw that Tosha's ice-cream shop was buttoned up tight. Ricardo's souvenir shack was still shuttered. She leaned over her counter and looked sideways toward Bernie's Boardwalk Fries and Hank's Hot Dogs. Nothing. No one. The midway was deserted.

Gus glanced at the wall calendar and the clock. "I'm not crazy, am I? It's Friday, July nineteenth, eight thirty in the morning and I'm making doughnuts. Maybe the rest of the world's crazy or sleeping in or the Point Bridge sank into the bay after I crossed it."

She shut off a beeping oven timer and pulled out a rack of cupcakes.

And then it hit her.

The vendors were not showing up. Purposely not opening their food and souvenir stands. This was their big move to prove their value to the Hamiltons. The plan they had cooked up at those meetings she wasn't invited to.

Although the vendors had begun to feel like the family she craved, that family had turned against her. And against the Hamiltons. Was this what Mel had alluded to when he suggested her loyalty would be tested?

Of all days. A busy Friday was one thing, but how did the other vendors know today was so important? She searched her memory. No way had she told them anything. Until Wednesday, she hadn't known bankers would be visiting the Point and acting on those appraisals. Her fellow vendors had stopped talking to her over a week ago. But somehow they'd chosen a day where their revolt would do the maximum damage. Catastrophic damage.

The phone rang, shattering the silence and making Gus jump. Her heart raced as she crossed the floor and grabbed it off the hook.

Evie's voice rushed loudly. "Gus, what's happening?"

"Trying to figure it out."

"You're the only vendor who's here. I'm sitting in Jack's office and we're looking at the security cameras."

"Should I wave?"

"Not funny." Evie's voice cracked and Gus heard tears in it.

"Sorry. I'm trying to understand what's going on. I got here extra early because I couldn't sleep. I've made hundreds of doughnuts and just realized I'm alone except for the employees getting the rides going."

"The park opens in less than an hour," Evie said.

"I know."

"So where are the other vendors? Are they all sick? Did they quit? Help me out here."

"I'm only putting two and two together, Evie, but I think they're boycotting."

"Boycotting?"

There was a muffled conversation, Jack's urgent tones railroading the quieter sounds of Evie, June and Virginia. She thought she heard something like Betty whining in the background. Probably too much noise and excitement for the old gal. It was too much drama for everyone concerned. The tense voices mixed with the feeling of white-water rapids in Gus's gut.

The next thing she heard was Jack's voice shouting in the background then right in her ear. "Gus, you better call up your friends and tell them to get in here and open those shops. I can't believe you did this to us. You tell them they're out on their butts if they're not up and running by ten. You tell them..."

Gus held the phone away from her ear. She set it down and gripped the table's edge, listening to a cacophony of voices from the receiver. Evie's and Jack's voices competed. The talking finally stopped and Gus put the phone back on its hook. She leaned against the counter, glancing at the clock, feeling sick. Rows and rows of fresh doughnuts lined up on parchment, waiting to be boxed or sold to hungry guests who would arrive in twenty-three minutes now. And no other food vendors would be operating.

She slid down and sat on the floor. *So Jack thinks I had something to do with this. He thinks my friends involved me in their decision to sabotage Starlight Point?* The clock ticked away several more minutes.

"Gus? Are you in there?"

She knew the voice. June Hamilton. The most neutral and possibly rational member of the family. She raised her hand and waved it, knowing June would see it over the counter. "Down here. Come in by the side entrance."

June strode through the door in three seconds, sinking down next to Gus.

"I don't know what to say," June began.

"You're not here for a doughnut?" Gus asked.

June leaned back against the counter and laughed. "Doughnuts go straight to my thighs and I have enough problems as it is right now."

"You sure do. You're probably sitting in

something sticky and those pants look like they're dry-clean only."

"Better than being in my dad's office right now. Evie is sobbing and Jack's stalking around yelling like a royal jerk. Mom is methodically brushing Betty—that poor dog will probably be bald by nightfall. I'm the only one doing anything useful."

"Which is?"

"Talking to you. You don't have to help us—you've got plenty of reasons why you wouldn't want to—but hear me out. Please."

"Listening."

"First off, sorry about my stupid big brother. I heard what he said on the phone. He's in full panic-the-plane's-going-down mode. Bankers will be here at nine thirty, want to do a walk-through starting about ten. All Jack can see right now is the mess the bankers are going to see and—I'm not gonna lie—the plane will go down."

"I know. Jack told me about the debts two nights ago when we—"

June almost smiled.

"When we were…uh…alone," Gus continued. "No one could have overheard."

"I don't know why the vendors chose today

to boycott, but you obviously didn't know about it because—duh—you're here. On behalf of my shouting brother, my sobbing sister, and my mother and her dog, I'm asking for your help."

"I'm not exactly on the vendors' good side," Gus said. "They didn't even invite me to their last three meetings. I think it's because, in their words, I've gotten too cozy with your brother."

"Smartest thing he's done all summer, if you ask me."

"I've only known the other vendors for a few months, but I thought they were my friends."

"And they left you out of this," June said, nodding. "That probably hurts, and I'm sorry to be here making it worse."

Gus sighed. "It does hurt. My family moved around a lot when I was growing up, but I always thought I belonged here. I want to make Bayside and Starlight Point my permanent home, build a business here."

June scooted closer to Augusta. "There must be some way to fix this. Some way we can reason with the other vendors."

"I know they're angry and upset about their

contracts, and they probably want to show Jack they're important. Make him appreciate them. Closing their shops for the day—or even part of the day if that's what they plan—would sure as heck make their point."

"And then some," June agreed.

"But they're not malicious. And they're dedicated to Starlight Point. They love this place—they've spent their lives here, some of them. That's why they're so mad. If their boycott puts the whole place in jeopardy..."

Gus got up and poured two cups of coffee. She sat down again and handed one cup to June.

"What the heck," June said. "I need something with this coffee." She stood and inspected the rows of doughnuts lined up on the counter, chose one with chocolate and sprinkles on top, and plunked down next to Gus.

They sat in silence as June tore into the pastry.

"I just don't think they could have known about the bankers' meeting today. The only people who knew were your family and me. And I didn't tell anyone."

"I know you didn't," June said. "That's why I'm asking for your help now."

Gus pulled her cell phone out of her apron pocket. “I’m going to start making phone calls. It might take some convincing and some time, but I’ll do everything I can to get them in here.”

The opening bell sounded and excited voices moved their way. The first rush of people who’d been waiting outside the gate started pouring past. Families, teenagers, senior citizens with season passes and exercise on their minds. All of them expecting to see the food stands and souvenir stands open as they made their way toward the rides. Gus was glad she couldn’t see their confusion as they passed her stand, but she knew she had to get up and put on a brave face.

A summer employee, Becky, rushed through the side door, breathing heavily.

“Sorry I’m late. Kid problems. My daughter didn’t want to wear…” Becky stopped, looking around at the rows and rows of doughnuts and June Hamilton sitting on the floor under the counter with Gus. “What’s going on?”

“Tell you in a minute. First, toss on an apron and start selling doughnuts and coffee. We’re the only game in town right now, and it’s going to be a wild morning.”

Gus walked out the side door with June. “Any way you can convince the bankers to start their tour at the back of the park? Go through the hotel first and then the Wonderful West? Only vendor in the hotel is me, and I know Liz will be there. Aren’t nearly as many vendors in the Wonderful West, so it won’t be as obvious back there.”

June hugged Gus. “Good idea. I’ll see what I can do.”

“Try to give me until noon before you bring them to the main midway.”

“I’ll try. Thanks. I really mean that.”

“And brush the doughnut crumbs off your blouse.”

June looked down and laughed. “I should’ve stayed in New York,” she said. “I can’t handle the excitement here.”

TOSHA ANSWERED HER cell phone on the first ring. “Hello, Gus. I bet I can guess why you’re calling—and I can understand if you’re mad we left you out…”

“I’m not mad about that,” Gus said.

“Really?”

“Upset maybe, but not mad. I get it. You were afraid I’d tell Jack. Evie would sure find out about a boycott if I didn't assign any workers to my shops or bake anything in advance. I get it, Tosha."

"So… I'm almost afraid to ask. What did Jack say when he saw none of us were showing up? Not that I regret it. He's got it coming. The way he's treated us this year…"

"Listen. Your point is made. Believe me, it's made. But Starlight Point is in trouble."

"Sure it is. Hungry people are gonna want fries, dogs and ice cream. They can't eat cookies all day long—even as good as yours are."

"It's more than that. You know those appraisers that have been hanging around?"

"Humph."

"They were appraising *everything* at the Point. Not just vendors. The whole place. Every ride, restaurant, flower garden and restroom. Bankers are here today, walking through the park, trying to decide if they'll extend their loans or foreclose on Starlight Point."

Dead silence for five seconds.

"Are you there, Tosha?"

"I can't believe— Starlight Point is in debt?"

"Yes, and it's serious. I heard inklings earlier this summer, but the Hamiltons keep to themselves about business. I just learned the whole story two days ago. And now the bankers are here. They start their tour at nine thirty. They want to see a healthy, thriving place or they could shut the whole thing down."

"I had no idea. I thought something was going on because I heard Evie tell Liz she was taking the nineteenth for family business. Thought we'd mess with their business a little, but we didn't know bankers were coming through. You gotta believe me."

"I do believe you, but we have to do something," Gus said.

"Sure do. You get off the phone. Go roll up the front awnings on all our shops. Turn on the signs. Get someone behind the counter. At least make it look like we're in business."

"What are you going to do?"

"I'm going to call everybody and get them there just as fast as they can."

"I've got June stalling the bankers. Think we've got till noon before they come up front. If we're lucky."

"Gus… I'm sorry I didn't trust you, wasn't sure which…"

"Just get all the vendors here. We'll talk about it later. Today, we're all on the same side."

Gus left Becky to run her shop alone, despite the chaotic crowd of hungry people. She grabbed her two other employees and headed for the row of shops across the midway.

She tried the side door on Ricardo's souvenir shop. Locked. She ran over to Tosha's. Also locked.

"Dangit," she said.

"Why do women always say that when I show up?"

Gus stopped shaking the doorknob and turned around. Mel Preston. With a huge ring of keys.

"Don't even have to waste time filling me in," he said. "June called me. Said I should do anything you said. I'm willing, but I'm still hoping for a doughnut out of this."

"Later. I'll make you doughnuts that will have you on your knees. Right now, I need you to open the doors, roll up the awnings and turn on the neon signs for all the vendors on the midway."

"Got it."

"Know any maintenance guys who can make hot dogs or scoop ice cream? Run a cash register?"

"Probably quite a few of them. Most of us

started off working at the food stands when we were teenagers. I worked two summers for Bernie's Boardwalk Fries." He cracked his knuckles. "I think I can still pull it off. I'll get on the radio and find someone for each of the shops."

"You're a lifesaver."

"Saving my own skin and everyone else's. Bank decides to call in their loans, we're all on the same sinking ship."

Twenty minutes later, it looked as though every stand on the midway was open. They also looked incredibly busy because long lines spooled out front. Gus speed walked from one stand to the next, checking on the progress.

A gray-haired maintenance man she'd seen around all summer wore a bright pink apron and wielded an ice-cream scoop at Tosha's.

"Having the time of my life," he said. "Haven't done this since I was seventeen. Can't believe how much prices have gone up since then, though."

Gus glanced at the long line of wiggling kids and exasperated parents. "I'll try to get someone to help you," she said.

At Bernie's Boardwalk Fries, Mel wore a

red apron and whirled from the fryer to the front counter, serving up orders of fries at roller-coaster speed.

"How much longer?" he asked when Gus walked in the side door. "I forgot how hard this is. I burned my finger and I'm sweating like I'm in hell."

"Bernie called. Stuck in traffic on the Point Bridge."

"Everyone's coming to the Point on a nice day like this," Mel said. He shook his head and turned back to the fryer.

Hank was the first vendor to arrive. He barreled down the midway, tossing on his condiment-stained apron, and took over behind the counter.

"I knew this was a bad idea," he said, shaking his head at Gus. "Should've told you what was going on."

"Can't talk about it now. Gotta move."

Gus grabbed the electrician who'd been manning the hot-dog stand and pulled him toward Ricardo's. "You can run a cash register, right?"

"I can take one apart and put it back together again."

"You're hired. Start selling hats and T-shirts.

Ricardo will be here in fifteen minutes, but people are lined up already."

"I'll sure try. Might look a little funny with my boots and tool belt."

"Throw on a Starlight Point T-shirt. You'll be fine."

CHAPTER TWENTY-FOUR

By noon, things were shaping up on the midway, and there was a chance visitors would be convinced that Starlight Point was having a successful summer's day.

Gus was glad the bankers had taken their time coming up the trail from the Wonderful West. Because of the makeshift crews at the midway vendors, the food lines were long and rowdy. Little by little, the vendors and their usual crews replaced the maintenance guys and handled the lines of customers.

At Aunt Augusta's Midway Bakery, business was booming. Thanks to her sleeplessness, Gus had stockpiled a doughnut supply that lasted a good half hour, enough to make a dent in the demand for food and give the other shops a fighting chance to get moving.

Gus shaded her eyes, standing on the hot white concrete in front of her shop. She saw them. A pack of dark-suited men with a very tall man in the middle. Behind the group, a woman with a red wagon dodged in and out of the crowds. *Betty's sure having an interesting day*, Gus thought. She just hoped Jack remembered to slow his pace.

Gus didn't know why she continued to wait outside her bakery, watching the group make their way past the Silver Streak, Kiddieland and the entrance to the Sea Devil. They lingered in front of the new ride, and Gus thought they might use their VIP status to bypass the two-hour line and take a whirl on the sea monster. But they didn't. Perhaps Jack was trying to sell the ride as a great investment. Now that it was running well, maybe it was.

Snowflakes swirled through her insides as she waited for them to get closer. She just wanted one glimpse of Jack's face and then she'd retreat inside her bakery and hide in the back. The crowd parted a little. Even from fifty feet away, Gus could see that Jack didn't look happy. Evie wore a strained smile. Virginia walked along, head down, dragging Betty's wagon.

June, however, had the arm of one of the bankers and was smiling broadly and pointing at things as they passed. She seemed to be the only Hamilton who didn't want the pavement to open up and swallow her.

Time to escape into her bakery. Gus took one step and someone tapped her on the shoulder.

"Aunt Augusta?"

She whirled around. A blonde girl who couldn't be more than sixteen stood before her in her bright yellow sweeper costume. She was one of the many teenagers whose job was walking the midways with a broom and dustpan whisking away cigarette butts, food wrappers and other trash.

The girl held a white bakery box. Gus smiled while her insides sunk. *Not now.* Since the STRIPE training classes, she'd seen a dozen cakes made by employees who were proud of their new skill. They didn't *have* to show her their cakes, they *wanted* to show her. Wanted her approval. Every time, she had assured them it was wonderful while thinking how nice it was to belong somewhere, to be valued.

But this was no time for cakes, not with Jack and the bankers closing in.

"I made a cake," the girl said, unaware of the day's drama. She held out the box.

Gus took it, glancing over her shoulder. The banker group was closing in fast. There was no way she could avoid Jack now. Not that she had anything to fear. He was the one who'd jumped to conclusions, the one who'd accused her of ratting him out to the other vendors. He was the one who should apologize.

But not now. Not in front of the bankers. She'd have it out with him later.

"Let's see," Gus said, opening the box and managing an encouraging tone. The white cake had a bright yellow sun in the middle. In green icing, it said *Please Don't Litter.* The border was a neat row of alternating yellow and green dots.

"Beautiful!" Gus said.

"Nice cake," a man in a dark suit added. He was peering into the box, smiling. "My wife is a cake decorator. Works from home making wedding cakes. You should see some of them. Amazing hard work."

The sweeper blushed, smiling at the man and Gus.

"Why did you bring a cake to work? Are you having a party?" the man asked.

"It's from the STRIPE," the girl said.

"STRIPE?"

Jack towered over them now, the whole group halted by the cake. "The Summer Training and Improvement Plan for Employees," Jack said. "Every summer our employees can learn an interesting and useful skill. In the past, it's been everything from car repair to square dancing. This year, it's cake decorating." His tone was neutral, almost flat.

The banker clapped his hands, grinning. "I love it. Man, I can't wait to tell my wife about that. She'll get a kick out of it." He turned back to Gus and gestured at her apron. "Are you the cake-decorating teacher?"

"Among other things, yes. I run three bakeries here at the Point, but my flagship store is over in Bayside."

Virginia stepped into their circle. "Augusta is one of our lease vendors. We're really lucky she found time to teach our STRIPE classes this summer on top of running her bakeries."

The banker nodded. The other men in suits stepped closer. "Tell me more about the lease-vendor program here," one of them said.

June put an arm around Gus and smiled. "How about you hear it from a vendor?" she said. "Do you mind?" she asked Gus.

Gus glanced at Jack, but he stared at the

ground, the awning over her shop, the cable cars overhead. Anywhere but her.

"I'd be glad to tell you about it. I'm the newest one here, so I've had some learning to do myself. Many of the other vendors have been here for decades."

"That's hard to believe," another of the bankers said. "Decades?"

Gus nodded. "Yes. They have a lot of loyalty." Jack's head came up and he finally looked her in the eye. She couldn't read his expression.

"The baker who had the contract here for the last twenty years retired, so I saw this as a great opportunity. For a flat fee and a percentage of profits, we lease one or more locations within the gates, the majority of them along this midway. Most of the vendors are quick-service food like hot dogs, fries and ice cream. A few are souvenir stands like Ricardo's—" she pointed across the midway "—selling Starlight Point hats and T-shirts."

"And you said you had three? Do all the vendors have more than one?" a banker asked.

"I'm the only vendor with three this year. This location," she said, gesturing at her pink awning, "one in the Wonderful West and one in the lobby of the hotel. Maybe it's too ambitious, but people like sweets wherever they are, I think."

"From a business standpoint," one of the bankers asked, turning to Jack, "wouldn't you be better off taking over these stands and running them yourselves? You could control product and profit more."

"I've thought about that," Jack said, his face relaxing and his shoulders dropping just a little. "But the vendors make things a lot more interesting around here. Many of our guests who've been visiting for years expect to get a Hank's hot dog."

"Or Bernie's boardwalk fries," June added.

"Or Tosha's homemade ice cream," Evie said, slipping into the circle and smiling broadly at Gus.

"They provide the kind of variety we'd probably lose if we ran everything ourselves. And I'm quite partial to our newest vendor," Jack said, inching closer to Augusta. "I have a serious sweet tooth."

"Want to see my Starlight Point–themed cookies?" Augusta asked. She put a little distance between herself and Jack, hoping it would help her figure out his mood.

The bankers followed Gus to her front

counter. “Becky, can you put one of each of the Starlight Point designs on a tray?”

“Be just a minute,” she replied.

“I’ll help her,” Evie said, slipping around to the side door. “Looks like she’s got her hands full.”

“Evie works for me, managing my hotel location and my books. I couldn’t do without her.” Gus leaned against her counter. “It’s about lunchtime,” she said. The bankers ringed her in, looking like kids whose mother had promised them cookies fresh out of the oven. “I’ll bet you’re hungry.”

“Starved,” one of them said. “I’m thinking of trying a Hank’s hot dog and some—what’d you call the fries?”

“Bernie’s boardwalk fries.”

“Sounds good to me,” another banker said.

Jack stood just outside the shade from the awning. She had no idea where their relationship was going after their earlier conversation, but they would have to figure that out later. Without so many witnesses.

Evie shoved a parchment-lined tray across the counter. “Here we go. Aren’t these cool? We have the Lake Breeze Hotel, the new Sea Devil, the classic Silver Streak, a carousel horse, a few of the kiddie rides and older coasters, the night skyline and my brother's favorite, the Star Spiral."

Jack coughed. "Actually, I like them all. I was lucky enough to be one of the first taste testers before we opened for the year."

Gus picked up the tray, offering it to the bankers, but slipping the night skyline into her hand. She circled closer to Jack and handed him the cookie. His fingers gripped hers for a second and he leaned down to whisper, "I'm sorry."

"You can make it up to me later," she whispered back. "But I'm not going to make it easy for you."

The bankers took two cookies each and ate them right there on the midway. Gus thought they looked much happier than they had when they'd first approached. Guests going by paused and looked at the men in suits munching cookies. Jack ate the night skyline cookie in one bite.

Gus laid the ravished tray back on the counter.

"How about lunch?" Jack suggested to the group. "I'm buying dogs and fries."

The bankers moved off, but Evie stayed

behind. “Aren’t you having lunch with your guests?” Gus asked.

“In a minute.”

“How’s the visit going?”

“Better now,” Evie said. “Thanks to you. I’m sorry I was so hysterical when I called this morning. I had no idea what was going on, but I knew you’d fix it.”

“I patched it. But your family needs to work out a long-term relationship with the vendors that everyone can live with. I doubt I’ll ever get the maintenance guys to make fries or serve ice cream again.”

Evie laughed. “Wish I’d seen that.”

“Get a bottle of wine and rewind the security cameras. You won’t be disappointed.”

Evie hugged Gus and hurried to join her group, grabbing Betty’s wagon handle and hauling her along.

CHAPTER TWENTY-FIVE

THE AFTERNOON SUN burned overhead as Gus loaded her van and rolled the short distance down the docks to the Bayside Pavilion. Her aunt rode along to help wheel the wedding cakes inside quickly so the heat wouldn't melt the icing roses. As they backed down the long driveway to the kitchen entrance, Gus was reminded of the early-May evening she'd first met Jack.

Gus and her aunt had spent all day Saturday on the cake that would serve nearly five hundred wedding guests. On a busy weekend, Gus should have been at Starlight Point. But the used freezer she'd believed was a good buy had failed, and the prebaked layers were wrecked before anyone realized what had happened.

It was a disaster. At least it *would* have been a disaster if not for the healthy cash infusion from her bakeries at the Point. Strong cookie sales meant she didn't have time for setbacks, but the profits also allowed her to buy a new freezer for her flagship store.

If—*when*—Aunt Augusta's Downtown Bakery was strong enough to survive on its own, would she give up her shops at Starlight Point? Gus glanced across the water and her eyes followed a coaster train as it crested the hill on the Silver Streak and raced down. She'd come back to Bayside in search of the home she hungered for, and Starlight Point was a major part of that dream. She couldn't imagine a life without it.

Gus left the van running, air-conditioning blasting, while she ran to the kitchen to get the rolling cart. With her aunt's help, they maneuvered the five circular layers of the main tower and the four smaller layers for additional servings inside.

"This will sure be beautiful when it's done. Want me to stay and help set it all up?" her aunt offered.

Gus shook her head. "Nope. This is my favorite part. I have plenty of time and everything I need." She squeezed her aunt's shoulder, noting the tired lines of her face.

"Wouldn't mind sitting down and watching my talk shows I recorded. Been a long week for me."

"How about a ride back up the hill to your car?" Gus asked.

"I'm not that old. Never know, I might get a better offer between here and there if I walk slow enough. Call me if you need anything."

The older woman started to walk away, but Gus stopped her and hugged her.

"Thank you. For everything," Gus said. "I couldn't have done this without you."

"Make a cake? You could do that in your sleep," her aunt said.

Gus smiled. "Not just the cake. Thanks for making this feel like my home. And for believing in me. Even when I do crazy things like open four bakeries."

Aunt Augusta patted her cheek. "This has always been your home."

Gus walked her aunt as far as the van, loaded the rolling cart with extra flowers and decorating supplies, then headed in to build the cake, layer by rose-covered layer. It took her over an hour of placing a layer, adding pillars, setting another layer and filling in with borders and icing roses. She finally stood back, rolling her aching shoulders and surveying her work.

Fantastic. If no one knocked the cake table in the next hour, the bride and groom were going to be very happy.

The photographer had promised Gus copies of his professional photos of the cake, even offering her some enlargements for the walls of her downtown bakery. She'd befriended him by handing out his business cards and sending a few weddings his way. *Good business*, she thought. All part of her dream to make Bayside her permanent home.

Gus packed up her supplies, loaded the cart and rolled out to her van. Now that the cake was done, she finally had time to think about Jack. And the vendors. The tumultuous events of the day before seemed as if they were weeks ago, but she could still hear Jack's angry voice in her ear. That Friday-morning phone call still stung as though it was five minutes ago.

Evie had called earlier to ask her to attend a Tuesday-morning meeting with all the vendors. Obviously, both sides needed to talk about what had happened. Cooling off for a few days made sense.

She and Jack had a lot of talking to do, too.

The night birds were beginning their song,

promising a beautiful summer evening. Gus left the kitchen and walked toward her van. When she got closer, she saw another vehicle completely blocking her in. A hideous brown-and-tan SUV.

Jack leaned against the door of his car, arms crossed over his chest, smiling uncertainly.

"Looked for you at the Point," he said, shoving off the side of his car and opening the back doors of her van for her. "All three of your bakeries. Twice. I was afraid you were never coming back."

Her heart picked up speed. Seeing Jack was even sweeter than the giant cake she'd just made.

"I've been working all day getting this cake done."

"Last-minute job?"

She laughed. "Shouldn't have been. My freezer conked out and all the layers I'd prebaked got ruined. Stuff on the upper shelves melted and dripped on them. Had to do it all over again." She sat on the back bumper of the van. "Sometimes owning a business is a real pain in the butt. Did you know that?"

He sat next to her. Wrapped an arm around

her. Turned her face with the other hand and kissed her softly on the lips.

"I owe you a year's worth of apologies," he said. "I'd be willing to deliver one every day until you forgive me."

Gus laughed. "You'd probably be hoping for a piece of cake or pie each time you delivered."

"That would sweeten it for me," he said. "Even though I don't deserve it. I am sincerely sorry for what I said on the phone. I never believed you would betray me, but I was in panic mode."

"Panic mode is no way to make friends. But I forgive you anyway. Being the boss is a lonely job. That's why I'm here on a Saturday."

"But you're not alone. And you're done for the day," he said. "Right?"

Gus nodded.

"And you have an empty stomach."

"Had an early lunch at the shop. Hours ago. I'm starving."

"Perfect."

"Are you asking me to dinner, Jack?"

"Nope."

"Okay. What?"

"It's going to be a beautiful night."

Gus glanced at the bay, sparkling in the late-afternoon sun. "I can see that."

"Perfect for riding coasters at the Point."

Gus didn't answer. She got up and unloaded the metal cart, slowly arranging the back of her van. Jack leaned on the open door, where she had to brush against him every time she moved anything. They were right back where they'd first met, but a lot had happened since then. What happened next?

"You haven't said yes yet," Jack commented. "I could sweeten the deal with a VIP pass. No waiting in line for any of the coasters."

"Are you kidding? The long line is where I build up my nerve. It's part of the experience."

She wiped off the empty cart slowly and methodically.

Stalling.

Resisting.

Wanting Jack, but fearing wild rides. She'd been on an emotional one lately.

"Also got a pretty convenient parking space right at the gate."

"Are you trying to impress me?"

"Yes."

Gus sighed and looked him in the eye.

"Can we start small? I've only been on one ride this whole summer."

He grinned. "Which one?"

"Very funny."

"If you liked it, I could arrange for another private ride."

"Starting slow tonight, remember?"

"Whatever you want," Jack said. "How about you park the pink beast, I'll meet you behind your bakery and we'll go from there."

"I HAD NO idea this is what you meant when you said you wanted to start small." Jack grimaced next to her. His knees were up to his chin on the small seat of the old-fashioned cars.

"I like these," Gus said. She honked as she looped over a bridge, passing a little kid driving his bored-looking dad. "You should have sat in the back where there's more room."

"Then I couldn't do this," he said, putting his arm around her shoulders and pulling her in for a quick kiss.

"Quit that. Gotta keep my eyes on the road. They throw you out if you bump the car ahead."

Jack rolled his eyes. "I'm almost afraid to ask what's next."

"I'm thinking of going big. Bumper cars."

"Are we ever going to get to the Sea Devil?"

"Eventually. I like to build up the anticipation. It's more fun that way."

Jack squeezed even closer on the tiny seat. "I'm not sure how much longer I can wait."

Gus looked straight ahead, driving carefully into the loading station, never so much as touching the car ahead. She unbuckled them both and climbed out, taking Jack's hand and pulling him to a stop right outside the ride exit.

"I'm ready for the roller coaster now, Jack."

"Really? The Sea Devil? Or at least the Silver Streak?"

"Yes. On one condition. You tell me what's going to happen at the Tuesday-morning meeting."

"Aren't you planning to come?"

"Maybe. But I'm getting my new freezer delivered."

Jack looked confused. "Can't it be delivered later in the day?"

Gus shook her head slowly. "They'll call me Monday night with a four-hour window for Tuesday. I have to plan my day around it."

"Those jerks. Their windows are always such a tease."

Jack took her arm and headed for the midway, where the Sea Devil squatted menacingly. "To answer your question, I think you'll like what I have to say at the meeting."

"Why do you think so?"

"Because I'm taking the excellent advice offered to me by someone very special."

"And that is?"

"Be honest. Try some open communication. I'm going to lay out details for the lease vendors, offer a compromise on this year's contracts and be up-front about next year's. I just hope they'll be in a forgiving mood."

"I think they will," Gus said. "How about the bankers?"

Jack considered his answer. "I don't know about forgiving, but I think they're at least fair. We've got a chance to prove ourselves, and that's all we can ask for right now."

They walked under the steel structure of the new ride. "We're here." Jack sorted through a key ring, opened a narrow gate and led Gus right onto the platform for the ride. "Here's a little secret. This ride isn't nearly as wild as our advertising has suggested. It's just a half step up from the Silver Streak, despite all the hype."

"I had a dream about that," she said.

"What?"

"A dream. You and me, riding the Silver Streak endlessly, laughing and laughing."

"Was this before or after our ride on the Star Spiral?"

Gus thought for a second. "Before."

"So you've been thinking about me for a while," he said, grinning. "I'm pretty hard to resist."

Gus slugged him on the upper arm. "Get over yourself, Jack."

The ride hostess stepped over. "Ready, Mr. Hamilton?"

"If my guest is."

Gus nodded. "Ready."

They climbed into the seats and pulled down their shoulder harnesses.

"Best ride up here in the front. I promise," Jack said, speaking right into her ear so she could hear him over the ride operator on the loudspeaker, who was giving directions and counting down to launch. "If you hate it, I'll drive you straight home and hold your hair while you puke. I'll even tuck you into bed."

Gus didn't have time to answer. The rapid-launch system flew them into the clutches of an evil sea monster that spun them around the track, up and down hills, slowed them down, and relaunched them into a series of tight curves and loops. She started screaming on the first hill and never stopped.

It was the most exhilarating two and a half minutes she'd ever had on a ride. Not counting the Star Spiral. They jerked to a stop outside the station and Jack twisted his body to see her in the dim evening light.

"Gus, you okay? Can't tell from your screaming if you loved it or hated it."

She took a deep breath and waited for her spinning head to come to a stop. "Loved it."

They waited for the shoulder harnesses to release. Jack sprang up, taking Gus's hand and helping her onto the platform.

He kissed her in front of everyone waiting to get on the ride. Loud applause and whistling cheered them on until the station operator got on the loudspeaker. "Happens all the time, folks. Nothing more romantic than surviving a terrifying sea monster. Now, Mr. Hamilton, if you'd move along..."

Jack grinned and waved to the ride operators and the people on the platform. He held Gus's arm as they descended the steps.

"Thanks for trusting me and taking a chance."

"I'd do it again."

They walked out the beach entrance, hand in hand. The sunset was over, and lights were on all over Starlight Point. Jack leaned against the rail and drew Gus into his arms, not leaving a sliver of space between them.

"I'm sorry," he said.

"Why? I liked the ride. And the kiss was pretty good, too."

"Not that. I'm sorry I didn't open up sooner, tell you what shape the Point is in. I thought I could make it better if I just kept it to myself. I was wrong."

"Totally wrong. But understandable. And you're doing the right thing now."

"Thank you. I can't thank you enough. You saved us by opening the stands and calling in the vendors. I knew you'd throw me a life ring if I needed it."

"Yes," she said, smiling.

Their kiss was long and slow as the lake breeze washed over them. He pulled back, rubbing the pads of his fingers gently down her cheeks. "There's something I need to share with you. Maybe the timing's not right, but I can't wait. I'm ready now."

Gus felt the same rush of emotion she'd encountered on the roller coaster. Whatever he was about to tell her, she knew she was going to like it.

"Say it, Jack. I'll even ride the Sea Devil again if you want."

"Come to the hotel."

"Okay." Her heart raced. "But you have to give me some clue."

He smiled broadly. "It involves cake."

Gus dropped her hands from his shoulders. She willed her eyes to lose their stupid dreamy look.

"I finally made one. Want to show it to you."

"Oh," Gus said.

Great. Another cake. Just when she thought she and Jack might crest over the hill, they were getting buckled up to look at a birthday cake.

"It'll just take a minute," Jack said. "And then we'll go ride whatever you want."

Gus walked alongside Jack as if her legs were made of stone. Fine. She'd take a look at his stupid cake. It had better be good.

JACK WASN'T SURE if he should laugh or apologize. The disappointed look on Gus's face told him what he needed to know. He nodded politely at the young man who opened the hotel door. They crossed the shining hardwood floor of the lobby and swung through the bakery door. Evie was behind the counter.

"There you are!" she said. "Time for my break. Good luck, Jack. I hope Gus likes your cake." She snapped the sign to Closed and shut the door behind her, leaving Jack and Gus alone in the bakeshop.

"They're in the fridge in back," he said.

"I imagined. I do know my way around here."

"Sit down. I'll bring them out."

"Them?"

"I needed more than one."

Jack raced to the fridge and was back in a second with a cupcake in his broad hand. He hoped she wouldn't notice his hands shaking.

"It's a cupcake. And it says *I*," Gus said. "That's not a cake."

"Bear with me. I'm going for a different vision here."

Gus raised an eyebrow and Jack set the

cupcake in front of her on the table. "I'll get the next one."

A slow smile started across Gus's face, but he didn't stay to see it finish. He dashed for the fridge and ran back, his heart racing.

This cupcake said *love* in red letters. "I had to really work to fit that on," he said, setting it next to the first cupcake.

"Nice job," Gus said. Her tone was light, but a deep flush spread across her cheeks. "What do you love, Jack? Roller coasters? Sunshine? Cookies?"

"Be right back."

When Gus saw the next cupcake, she stared at it for a minute, lined up with the first two.

Jack waited, afraid to breathe, until Gus raised her eyes to his face and he saw the tears sparkling in them.

"Thanks for spelling out *you* instead of just using the letter *u*," she said, her voice shaking.

"You're worth it."

"I love you, too." She stood and opened her arms. "You had me at *love*," she said and sniffed. "It's not easy writing big words on cupcakes."

"Nothing worthwhile is easy," he said, pulling her close. "I love you. I've been falling in love with you since we met."

He kissed her, exploring her lips as if he had all the time in the world.

"There's a lot of summer left," he said, touching his forehead to hers. "I want to spend all of it with you."

Gus giggled, running her fingers through his hair and ruffling it. "My aunt says Starlight Point is a lover's paradise. Are you thinking about a summer romance?"

"I'm thinking about a lot more than that. If you're willing."

She kissed him, her hand on the back of his neck. "A summer romance is a good start, but I'd like to stick around and see where this ride is going."

"Deal."

The shop door swung quietly open. Evie peeked in. "Okay to come in now?" She crossed the floor and hugged Gus and her brother at the same time. "I knew you two were perfect for each other."

"Because he has a sweet tooth and I'm a baker?"

"That's right. Can't think of any other reason," Evie said.

"Wait a minute," Gus said, turning to Jack and grimacing. "Does this mean you're going to expect free cookies all the time? If so, we need to talk about my contract."

Jack glanced at his sister. "My partners and I did discuss contracts before June left for New York. Evie told us you and the other vendors made up."

Gus nodded. "Thank goodness. They've become like family to me."

"Could we persuade you to be our new liaison in charge of vendor relations?" Jack continued. "You've got a real talent for bringing people together."

"It's the frosting. No one can resist."

Jack ran a finger down her cheek and toyed with a piece of her hair. "It's a lot more than that. Will you take the job?"

"I don't know," she teased. "I'll think about it. Right now, I'm getting in line for a ride."

"Now?"

"Think there's a long line for the Star Spiral? We've got some unfinished business there."

Jack grinned at her. "Not if I can help it. Right behind you."

He followed Gus from the bakery then ran back five seconds later to grab two cupcakes.

"In case we get hungry," he said, winking at Evie and rushing off after Augusta, the star-light kissing the lake as they raced down the beach.

* * * * *

Don't miss the next book in
Amie Denman's miniseries
STARLIGHT POINT STORIES,
available soon from
Harlequin Heartwarming!